FARUK ŠEHIĆ

UNDER PRESSURE

Translated from the Bosnian by Mirza Purić

istrosbooks

First published in 2019 by
Istros Books
London, United Kingdom www.istrosbooks.com

Copyright © Faruk Šehić, 2019

Published originally as *Pod pritiskom*, 2004 , this book contains additional material

The right of Faruk Šehić, to be identified as the author of this work has been
asserted in accordance with the Copyright, Designs and Patents Act, 1988

Translation © Mirza Purić , 2019

Illustrations and cover art: Aleksandra Nina Knežević
Typesetting: Davor Pukljak, www.frontispis.hr

ISBN: 978-1-912545-02-5

Printed by Pulsioprint, France/Bulgaria

This publication is made possible by the goodwill and generosity of a number of
readers across the globe, who gave support through Kickstarter.

It's complicated

With the exception of a few scenes which take place in Sarajevo, this book is set in what is now the Una-Sana Canton, traditionally known as Cazinska Krajina – the Cazin Marchlands. During the 1992–1995 war, around 200,000 people were driven into four tiny towns at the north-western tip of Bosnia. The pressure was off the dial.

Fikret Abdić, a former food-processing corporation manager, led a fratricidal insurrection in the region that cost some 3,000 lives. Having served two thirds of a 15-year sentence for war crimes, he is now the municipal mayor of the town in which he committed them. His supporters were colloquially referred to as the Autonomists (*autonomaši*).

The protagonists of the stories set in Krajina are soldiers of the Fifth Corps of the Army of Bosnia and Herzegovina. They are referred to as fighters, because that is what they called themselves.

A few words have been left untranslated – *that's our artillery prep*. These include *kafana* (boozer), *rakia* (fruit brandy), *pastirma* (pastrami), *burek* (mince pie), *sevdah* (a genre of Bosnian folk music). *Turbo-folk* is also a genre of music, but cannot be explained by any craft that we here possess.

The funny letters and digraphs are pronounced as follows: Č as in Charlie, Ć as in Cicciolina, Dž as in George, Đ as in Giovanni, Lj as in Lyudmila, Nj as in Benyamin, Š as in Shane, Ž as in Zhivago.

Mirza Purić

In the beginning was Eden, whence we were expelled.

We watched the clouds pile up above the hills below which the Una flowed into our town. At first they were light in colour, then they took on the muddy hue of dirty snow. The air was electric, as it always is before a summer torrent. We didn't like rain because it meant the end of bathing for the day, and it had to be hellishly hot the day after for us to muster up the courage to dip in again. Bathing in the river was the main summer ritual in our town. Life existed only for the sake of bathing. The calendar existed because of summer and water. The town smelt of river, of riverine greenery, of fish. Duck feathers were in the air, fish scales scattered on the riverbank. Smoke rose from barbecues in every corner, crates of beer were cooling in the water. On the other bank, on the roof of a house in progress, the wind outspread the tri-colour with the red star, and the towels tied below it to bring happiness and well-being to the house and its occupants.

When a cormorant appeared on Mallard Isle, somebody tried to stone him away. His feathers were greasy black. He submerged and emerged swallowing fish. The current took him far down the river from the Wooden Bridge, where swimmers tried to drive him away by shouting.

I dived into the river till I could dive no more. The moment I'd emerge onto the bank, which we'd cemented for more convenient walking, I'd climb onto the platform again, leap up as high as I could, bow to the river, straighten my body and delve in with all my might towards the murky blue bottom. It's peaceful and quiet down there, and soothingly cold. The fish would scatter before me every which way. I'd dive straight into a shoal of nase and the odd chub.

Everyone dived, in order to make the most of the day. Some wouldn't come out of the water at all, they splashed about in the shallows like walruses letting the stream take them to the waterfall which catapulted them to the Wooden Bridge, some hundred metres from our beach on the Quai.

The clouds are now dark and menacing. Peak voltage in the air. Heavy drops fall hard. Bathing ceases, everyone rushes out of the water, only a few bathers are still swimming. Rain picks up pace, the drops are larger and colder. Thin trees dance in the wind. The raindrops weigh down on their crowns, like when an umbrella is being closed. It's roaring, and bolts of lightning rend the sky like in the Bible. One should find a lee, wait for the downpour to abate and go home. The surface of the river is obscured by the liquid curtain. It is as if the rain decided never to stop.

A HIERARCHY
OF THINGS

Under Pressure

1.

They've brought us to the frontline. Mud and fog everywhere. I can barely see the man in front of me. We almost hold onto each other's belts lest we get lost. We pass between burning houses. The file trudges on alongside rickety fences. The mud sticks to our boots, stretches like dough. Lines seen for the first time are the best. Everything is new, unusual and hairy as fuck. Especially when you take charge of a position at night, and the next day, in daylight, you realise you're sitting on the tip of a nail.

Charred beams are falling off roofs, sizzling in the mud. We trudge up a big slope. The grass is slimy with fog. Whenever someone falls, he brings the file to a halt and, as a matter of course, curses a blue streak at the motherland and the president. The very thought that we would sleep out in the open flares up my haemorrhoids. The guide, a military policeman, brings us up to the top of the hump. Emir and I take a shallow trench in which we find: a mattress and a quilt, mud-smeared, and a few fags, smoked down to the filter, nervously stuck into the soil.

'Alright, lads! Freezin', innit?' a voice reaches us from the right-hand side.

'Come 'ere and we'll talk,' replies Emir lying on the mattress.

A silhouette approaches from behind.

Hops into the trench.

'I'm from the third battalion,' he tells us as we shake hands. 'Got a fag?'

I open a cigarette case full of Gales.

'Ain't they gonna see us if we smoke?' asks Emir.

'Nah. They're far from 'ere, and the fog's thick.'

Emir and I both light up, as if on command.

'Now then, what's the lie of the land?' I ask. 'Is it 'airy?'

'They ploughed the hill with shells earlier today. A fighter from the second company 'ad 'is cheek blown off by shrapnel. On Metla, a hump twice the size of ours, they 'ave a couple of ZiS anti-tank guns. They can shoot us like clay pigeons,' Third Bat-Boyo recounts slowly.

'So, survivors will eat with golden spoons, just like the president promised,' heckles Emir.

'Ain't as bad as it looks,' Third Bat-Boyo comforts him. 'Gotta die someday any road'.

Fear creeps into me like mould. It's shrapnel shave day tomorrow.

* * *

'Your life line is broken in two places. You'll be wounded twice, once severely,' a Gipsy woman told me on one occasion. Dževada tossed the beans, read them, concluded:

'A journey abroad is in your future, and glad tidings from afar.'

She'd tell that to everyone, since we were surrounded from all sides, and we wanted to escape the siege, that is, to travel abroad. "Glad tidings from afar," that would usually mean a girlfriend who happened to be outside the noose when the siege started, or relatives who lived in Germany and sent money.

I've laid down a hierarchy of things:

1. war
2. alcohol
3. poetry
4. love
5. war again

Favourite ditty: Bed, you wonderful device, sleeping in you feels so nice.

Stupidest quote: *War is delightful to those who have had no experience of it*, Erasmus of Rotterdam.

Favourite colour: Blue, all shades of.

Favourite book: *Plexus* by Henry Miller.

Favourite beverage: Home-distilled *rakia*.

Favourite weapon: Hungarian Kalashnikov, ser. no. SV-3059.

Favourite dish: A bottle of rakia and a packet of fags.

Favourite quote: *To become immortal, and then die*, Jean-Pierre Melville.

Unfulfilled wish: For shrapnel to scar my face, so I look like a badass when I walk into a bar.

Then I fell asleep under the muddy quilt.

2.

'Fiver says Steelio will make it across the field.'

'Does it count if 'e's wounded, or does 'e 'ave to be unscathed?'

'As long as 'e makes it to that white 'ouse.'

Steelio, thus nicknamed on account of his studded heavy metal leather bracelet, is lying behind an openwork concrete fence. He's covered his head with his hands. Fine concrete dust is settling on his hair. He's made it exactly halfway to cover. Bullets from an

M-84 machinegun hit the concrete posts, whizz through the gaps, stick into the ground. Steely gets up, takes a running start and is brought down by a burst. The gamblers are sitting underneath a quince tree deep in the lee of a four-storey house.

'Steely, you alive?'

'Alive my arse, 'e's not movin', 'e's not even groanin'.'

'Well it's 'is own bloody fault, nobody made 'im dash for it in daylight, coulda waited for nightfall,' the third observer gets a word in.

Steelio gets up again, moves his stumpy legs with all his might. It looks like he's running on the spot, but then he finally takes off from his starting position. His mullet wafts in the wind. The M-84 is doing its thing, but Steelio finishes like Ben Johnson.

'Go on, give us the fiver.'

'Fuck off.'

'Well, did 'e make it or what?'

''E did, yeah.'

'Fair and square?'

'Fair and square, yeah.'

'Absolutely romantic?'

'Absolutely romantic.'

Steelio, leaning on the cold wall of the house, takes broken cigarettes out of his pocket. With his shaky fingers he puts half a cigarette in his mouth and lights up. Fixes his hair. Flicks dust and soil off his fatigues. Blood returns to his face. Night falls like a trump card.

3.

Zgemba is flicking bits of human brain off the filo pie with his fingernail. He's tearing pieces off with his right hand, dipping them into salt and putting them in his mouth. With his left he's noshing on cottage cheese, from a white plastic bag splattered with a mixture of blood and brains. His mug is sooty from cartridge gas. In his lap he has a 7.62 mm light machinegun. Five minutes ago this trench was occupied by the autonomist rebels. A still warm corpse is hanging over the breastwork. A burst blew half of his skull off. I turn him on his back. From the inside pocket of his army green jacket I take out his wallet. I look at a passport-size photograph of him. He had a receding hairline. Large, melancholy eyes. With the sharp edge of the photograph I floss out bits of apple from between my teeth.

* * *

In the middle of the operation Deba lit a fire behind one corner of a house to dry his socks. He had left his rifle leaning against the wall at the other end of the house. The autonomists counter-attacked. They caught Deba alive and unarmed. Tied his hands behind his back with steel wire and shot him behind the shed.

* * *

That evening, after we were relieved, we went to a kafana. We drank at the expense of the Fifth Corps, meaning for nothing. Zgemba chucked blue diazepams into a pitcher of rakia. We lapped it up from large tumblers. The landlord brought meze – pastirma and cheese – on the house. He had a good-natured mug. He seemed a seasoned host and caterer. The waitress, a Romanian, complained to him that we were drinking for nothing. He reassured her. Her teeth protruded from under her lips, with large spaces in between like on a rake. She said she used to date a bloke from our brigade, whom they used to call Pekar. After a few litres of rakia we started trashing the place. We shot the mirror and the shelves lined with bottles above the bar. Muffled by the noise, a turbo folk number was cheeping from the stereo. I tried to hit a fly swatter that was hanging from a nail in the wainscoting. In the beer garden we scattered the plastic chairs and tables. We butt-stroked a few locals who spoke up against our actions. We disarmed three policemen, lined them up in front of a hairdressing salon. The landlord drove us in his Lada to the schoolhouse where we were stationed, ten kilometres from the kafana. It started pouring outside. The wipers were sliding across the windscreen like pressure gauge pointers. Nothing else of note happened that evening.

From the Haiku Diary

I got drunk and fell asleep on the wooden stall where Jagoda displayed her groceries, in front of the Austro-Hungarian residential building in which I lived.
I was wearing light shorts and a T-shirt.
Mother saw me from the toilet window.
They brought me in holding me by the arms.
Washed my face over the tub.
I felt like a foreign object within a foreign object.
I looked like a weary robot.

* * *

My hands were shaking as I drank coffee.
Opposite the house.
At pizzeria *Amfora*.
It was completely normal that my hands were shaking.
Common alcohol tremors.
The coffee slid down my throat.
Rinsed the smell of last night's beer and cognac.
It was day six of the war.
For the first time in my life I was a refugee.

* * *

In the toilet of the Café West I took off my Levi's and sold them to
the owner for a hundred million dinars.
The one million note had Nikola Tesla on it.
The five hundred thousand one had Josip Broz Tito.
Beer soon ran out.
One beer cost half a million.
We drank whisky.
The barman poured it from a five-litre bottle.
We didn't notice when night fell.
Outside, cold water was pouring from a crude drinking fountain.
Soaking the hot asphalt.
The smell of linden blossom.
Honey in the air.
That's all I remember.

* * *

For a morning that gives us the illusion of a fresh start...
Arrow-like rays of sunshine came in through the window
of the room above the Café Hajduk.
It was pleasant inside.
Warmth caught on the tips of my toes.
I put on fresh white boxers.
I took some notes and coins out of my jacket pockets.
I opened the window and reached out.
A fresh breeze blew into my face.
And that was no illusion.
I counted the marks.
The morning was made for that.

* * *

21 April 1992 (Tuesday), at 18:15, war started in my town.
In the garden of Café Casablanca I was drinking Sarajevsko beer.
I was wearing the latest model of Adidas trainers.
A pair of Levi's.
A down jacket.
I hid at my uncle's some thirty metres from the kafana.
He gave me a .357 Magnum and sixty rounds.
Which I put in my trouser pockets.
Some bullets had hollow points.
Those were the dum-dum bullets.
Shells and projectiles of various calibres were the soundtrack of the first day of war.
I saw a shooting star crash down across a piece of sky between the roofs of two
houses.
I made a wish.
For the war to end.
And to make up with my girlfriend.

* * *

'Ow much money 'ave you got?
Ten marks.
I've got five.
We can get pissed as newts.

* * *

We're drinking beer from the bottle.
The floor is made of marble.
It radiates cold.
It's sultry outside.
Nobody's wearing a watch.
Because time is utterly pointless.

* * *

It's wonderful being a refugee.
Means you're a fifteenth-class citizen.
And nobody knows you.
You can take a piss in the middle of the street.
And go on your way.
The passers-by will say: 'What an oik, a proper savage!'
'Why didn't they kill the lot of you?'
'Why didn't you fight?'
'Cowards!'
'Cunts!'
'Have you no balls?'
Only sometimes the 155 mm howitzer shells whizzing across the
sky remind them that there is no such thing as deep rear in this war.

* * *

A packet of Gales is 17 marks.
Partners are 20.
HBs cost 25.
Skopsko beer is 10 marks.

Ćevapi meatballs 20.
A sack of flour 1000 marks.
A kilo of coffee 330.
We're surrounded from all sides.
But, there's a substitute for everything.
Quince leaf can be smoked and costs zero marks.
Roasted rye coffee is a mark a kilo.
A bottle of reeky rakia is 10 marks.
Ćevapi are a luxury anyway.
Maize bread is tasty and cheap.
We're still surrounded from all sides.

* * *

At six in the morning my mother plucked dewy pigweed in the
nearby dales.
She brought the harvest home in her raised apron.
For dinner we had blanched pigweed with garlic, pigweed soup
and pigweed salad.
I'm full of iron.
As strong as Popeye the Sailor.

* * *

I loll about on a grey humanitarian aid sponge mattress.
Ants are marching up the wall in wide columns.
I'm popping 10-milligram diazepams.
Sleeping twenty hours at a time.
In my room I practise walking with crutches.

My wounded foot still hurts.

I'm reading T.S. Eliot's *Love Song of J. Alfred Prufrock*.

In the guest room Greta and Nađa are playing solitaire.

Mum is fiddling about with our wood-burning stove.

Dad is away on the frontline.

Behind our refugee house Mum planted onions, peppers, tomatoes.

We're waiting for the garden to produce produce.

In front of our doorstep, Humpy Horsie is happily barking.

The sun is at its zenith.

* * *

From the last dugout to the left they *wired* us that Osman Jakušović had been KIA.

A sniper hit him in the forehead, by the hairline.

It was impossible to reach the farthest dugout on Padež hill.

That night they brought him down on a stretcher.

He woke up from cardiac arrest.

He mumbled netherwords.

Our hair stood on end as we listened to the dead man talking.

They took him to the rear.

He died in hospital after three days.

I never got to know him well.

I don't remember his face.

He was a tall, muscular lad from the village of Stijena.

* * *

10 May 1992 (Friday)
Nothing has happened to me today.

* * *

The machinegun barks like a dog.
I've plucked a shirtful of cherries.
Bullets whizz above incandescent roofs.
They say a sniper's been at it from the Old Citadel.
Here and there, 60 and 82 mm mortars *operate*.
From time to time a tank shoots a shell.
A rocket launcher lets out a volley.
I shudder if something explodes nearby.
Shudders creep up the spine.
Palms sweat.
I'm talking about normal things.
Like clouds, cherries or the river Una.

* * *

I have decided to write sparsely.
End of war not in sight.
Mon. – drunk.
Tue. – drunk.
Wed. – ditto.
Thu. – o.

To Eternity

1.

The plan was quite simple: We would stretch out and form a firing line. The nine of us. The distance between each two fighters 5–10 metres. Frontal assault from the Standard Operating Procedures. Baldie will fire a rocket from his shoulder-fired Yugoslav Army Zolja launcher. That's our artillery prep. We will rise up from the grass. Start shooting and shouting the *Takbir* as we dash for their trenches. Whoever survives, survives.

Now we lie about and smoke in the safety of our own trenches. We're wearing our helmets, and our ammunition vests are stocked with thirty-round magazines. Baldie is slinging his Zolja over his back. Our mighty artillery. Faćo is the only one of us who has a rifle with a wooden stock. He says it's his lucky rifle. The trenchies are offering us cigarettes and coffee, eyes ablink with happiness because they're not participating in the operation. Everything for the commandos. Small talk, nobody mentions what is to come. As if we were going on a picnic, not a trench raid.

October wind musters out veteran beech and hornbeam leaves. As they fall, they brush leaf against leaf, rustling like Indian silk. The pines are indestructible. Their dark green needles comb the wind. We wait for the battalion commander to give the off via a Motorola. Night is in force. We're in the forest, where our strange firing line in the shape of a horseshoe is formed. Below the forest runs an asphalt road. Further down is a great big hollow, as dark as King Kong's gullet. Three hundred metres across the hollow our line continues. So we're bulging into their line. An un-fuck-with-able salient exposed to guns of all calibres.

Baldie motions us to move. Hafura and I go on a recce, just in case, although midnight blue is the colour-in-chief. We head out of the forest. We walk like camouflaged ghosts, and sneak up to a stretch of stunted undergrowth. If somebody opens up on us, we're fucked because we're between the lines. We can only move by ear. We hear indistinct human speech. We hold our breath. Some kind of tapping sound is coming from their trenches. Dull thuds. As if they're digging in. Now? What the fuck? Baldie approaches with the rest of the detail. We take up positions as planned and start to crawl. *Golo brdo.* Has there ever been a stupider name for a hump than Barren Hill? We close up to the spot. We can't see their trenches. It seems they are just below the brow of the fell, on the last slope. Baldie gets up, telescopes the Zolja out. He takes aim, eyeballs it. The rocket flies above the hill and on to Zanzibar. He must've hit a barn or some such strategically significant facility. Doesn't matter, it's just a psychological trick anyway. Explosions stoke fear, and fear makes you see things, your eyes pop out and gleam white, like those of an ox about to be slaughtered.

We dash, we shoot, we shout.

Metres seem like kilometres in a marathon race.

Time stretches like the rubber strips on a catapult.

Tracers fly every which way.

Enemy fire slows us down.

We just lie on the ground, without any cover.

That's it. *Golo brdo.* A dying range.

Hit the deck, graze the grass.

'Baldie, me gun's jammed, come over 'ere!' yells Faćo.

Baldie kicks his gun clear. Faćo puts the rifle's wooden stock in front of his face to shield his forehead.

'Fuckin' 'ell, it's a tough one!' I hear Hafura.

'Tits up, this. Pull back!' bellows Baldie.

No time to talk. We're rolling downhill towards our line. We're shielded from the bullets as we're just below the shoulder of the hill. Hand grenades explode in the place we were a second ago. The blasts ring out like in a well. We reach the forest. None killed, none wounded. The recruit hangs his head, stares at the ground. His pale complexion lends him the appearance of a zombie. His aquiline nose, hanging from his face like an upside down butcher's hook, turns him into a walking caricature. He bends over at the waist as he walks, as if to measure his insecurity with strides. To have a raw recruit in your unit is to be blighted by bad luck. It's incredible how death sticks to them. At times I was convinced I could make out the sigil of doom on their faces.

'All the king's 'orses couldn't take this fuckin' 'ill,' Hafura says.

'Yep, it's a tough one, fuck.'

'Night raids are a lottery,' Merva makes himself heard.

'Everything's a lottery: breakin' the lines, holdin' the lines, goin' about in mufti on leave, you can catch death wherever.'

'Nasty fuckin' business, this,' Baldie speaks up.

'To top it off, me gun keeps jamming', complains Faćo.

Baldie winks and smiles. We descend to the asphalt road.

'Right lads, see ya, then,' the guard from the dugout far left takes his leave of us.

We move in a group. We footslog like tin robots. We're going back two hundred metres towards our rear. When we get there, the house we're quartered in emerges from the murk. Merva and I take first watch. The others go to bed. We're standing in front of the door looking at the green in front of the house. To our right gapes a large hollow. Our positions are some half a kilometre up the mountain. For all intents and purposes, we're a picket. The dark thickens, like when a train suddenly flies into a tunnel.

'Tomorrow, I mean in the mornin', we'll be attackin' again, it seems.'

'Gettin' fucked is what we'll be doin'!'

'They've dug in down to the centre of the Earth, can't scratch 'em,' Merva moans to himself.

In the distance, a drunk is shooting tracers into the sky. I piss on the corner of the house. Live to fight another day. Me wanger.

2.

Same thing again. Only this time we're attacking by day. What was the sky like? Was it sunny? I don't remember. The uniform has a uniform unisex smell. The grass is wet and grey-green like the walls of a public lavatory. It is perfectly quiet those few minutes before the attack. The sounds of nature, too, die down. Or the brain doesn't register them, focused as it is on one thing only: staying alive.

My body is like a sweaty clenched fist. The firing of the Zolja. Some shooting and shouting of *Takbirs*. We've cracked their line with unexpected ease. Hopped into their empty trenches. A twitch crumples up my face. Expanding bullets are popping like popcorn. Redžo Begić is kneeling on my right. Stalks of straw jut out from under an army blanket. We rummage through some army bags we find there. The owner of the one I've got is called Duško Banjac. His name is written in pencil on a piece of paper from a graph pad. We stuff cardboard packets of ammo into our pockets. A jet of thick blood spurts from Redžo's mouth. He gurgles. His face assumes the hue of lye. At first I thought the bullet had gone through his mouth.

We get him out of the trench and further, some ten metres below it, to cover. His death took only a few seconds. We didn't even have time to bandage him. The bullet went through his chest from above. Ripped up his heart. We covered him with a shelter-half – when you see a dead man you're reminded of your own mortality.

The recruit retches and chucks up slimy morsels of undigested food. We leave him with the casualty to wait for CASEVAC to come from the rear and pick up the body. Fighters from the adjacent brigade have broken enemy lines on the right flank and burst into some houses level with Golo brdo. We're making our way through short stalks of un-harvested maize. A shell lands between Hafura and Husin. Both go airborne, together with mown off maize stalks. Husin is wounded in the left shin, a wound worth three or four months of leave. Hafura is blast-injured. Baldie radios in that we have two wounded and one dead.

There is no worse feeling than having to press on with the operation after a situation like this. Sickness and fear reach superhuman proportions.

We come across a body folded over the breastwork like a sack of flour. He's wearing former Yugoslav People's Army olive green coveralls. He is 30–35, has a long blond moustache and a new battle harness, which now has no bearing on his appearance. Blood is trickling down from his nostrils, as if he were a minor character killed in the first minutes of a cheap karate film. His wide open eyes stare at the rutted ground.

Thirty metres further on, we discover another corpse. This one is barely 19. He's lying on his back. His underpants are around his knees. With dignity or without, the man is dead. *No one flies off into the sky. The earth attracts bodies and lead.*

* * *

An hour later, Paden and I are prone behind a long berm. We're controlling a hundred-metre stretch of the meadow. Shells stick into the soil in front of and behind us. I feel one is about to splash onto my back any moment now. Their artillery covers every inch of the ground. I wish I were a mole now. Chickenly panic creeps into me. I wish I could slough off my body, become ethereal. Rid myself of flesh, blood and reason. Become a thin translucent zero.

In fear dwelleth God.

I don't pray to him, as the war has rendered his existence pointless. He is now most certainly in another galaxy. Snivelling in safety and solitude. Missing not a hair off his head. He's stacked himself up a breastwork of metal planets. Repeating his creation experiment, because solitude is nasty and he wants to socialise. He needs some new creation: Manotaurs. He's sick of humans. He has failed. Appalled, he has given up on the Earthlings. Shabby artist, that lad. Still, he did invent evil. If he ever existed.

Pieces of shrapnel, like Chinese stars, whizz all around us. If I saw myself in the mirror now, the shock would kill me. I change cover every now and then. I hop into a small depression, I get scratched in the wild brambles. Shells are landing there, too. Paden is calm. He's lying on his stomach, observing. From the rucksack on his back juts out the sword of a chainsaw. Below it, he tied a ghetto blaster to the rucksack straps.

''As that piece of rubbish got any batteries?'

'I wouldn't be luggin' it to battle if it didn't, would I now?'

'Find us some music, so we don't 'ear when a shell drops on us.'

Paden turns the radio on. He twists the plastic knob. Goes through stations playing classical music: Bach, Beethoven, Rachmaninov. Piano, organ, violins, bassoons and clarinets drive me schizo. Horror has an agent in every cell of my body.

'Fuck off with that jangle!' I shout to Paden.

The plastic dial moves on. Bowie's *Rock 'n' Roll Suicide* brings me to tears. I can see before my eyes a massive bar of solid wood. And a pint of foamy beer. A fluorescent lamp swaying above the bar, creating a sense of hovering. Everything is slowed down. Her greenish eyes sparkle, her lips swell pinkly before the kiss. I look at her face as we're kissing. It becomes deformed with beauty. *Give me your hand…* , Bowie sings. The flashback to peacetime is cut short like when the film snaps in the middle of the screening. The dial travels on. The search for salvation is a soap bubble. Radio Korenica is playing a song with the following lyrics:

Dvor na Uni, Dvor na Uni, quaint little church upon a hill
That's the place where, that's the place where Serbs are breeding still…

The song is ideal for both laughter and tears. But shells are still dropping, stretching the mind. Now and again we are reduced to a state of feeble-mindedness. The belts connecting the drive wheels in our heads keep falling off. The clatter of the tanks a kilometre ahead is the most unnerving sound on earth. It'll be the same thing again: squeeze your anus tight, shrink your brain to the size of a marble. We are lovely, innocent vowels spat out from the Devil's mouth. Carry out the orders with the precision of a guided rocket. Act by inertia like a stray bullet. Be part of a stained glass window where the dominant colour is that of human mince. Hail to the homeland! Eyes right! The thud of the marching step. Ironed flags fluttering. Polished pips on the epaulettes gleaming. Hearts tick-tocking like clockworks.

'Something's well dodgy. They should've relieved us yonks ago. Maybe they've pulled back and just left us 'ere?' Pađen thinks out loud.

'I suggest we slowly slope off. No point anyway…'

'Fuck the point! And fuck whoever invented it.'

'So, where do we go now?'

'No idea.'
'Crawl up our mums' fannies.'
'Best place to be.'
'What if they've counterattacked?'
'Then we're fucked.'

* * *

Baldie takes down the muster roll. Troop strength: nine men plus pen-pusher. Absent: one at barracks (pen-pusher). Wounded: two fighters. Dead: one. On med leave: one in psych ward (recruit). At muster: five fighters.

We drink rakia and smoke in silence. Outside, fog captures acres of territory. Statistics reigns supreme. With great confidence it handles surplus and shortage. It measures morale, weighs men like heads of cattle. Standard deviation, plus/minus infinity.

Now We Get a-Rude and a-Reckless

1.

We're digging up an Autonomist. Our razor-sharp shovels slice through the sloshy snow and stick into the makeshift mound. The soil is sodden sludge. The sound of metal stabbing the loamy clay breaks the winter silence. Around us, stunted spruces, dishevelled like Gremlins. They are slowly stripping off their overwhites as the snow thaws and falls to the ground with a thud. A southerly blows, but it's still cold. The hands dry and crack, the fingers tingle. A magpie, in his black and white kit, zig-zags overhead. We lean onto the shovels to get the unpleasant business over with. Half of the mound is gone, and the rest looks like a scab torn up by a surgeon's tweezers. Now and again, Beardo looks skywards, gets momentarily lost in thought, and then continues to dig. As if to apologise to the heavens for what he's doing.

'It's all the same to 'im now, nothin' bothers him anymore,' mumbles Beardo.

''E's not even a 'uman bein' anymore. Just a corpse,' I add. 'Just some body, arms, legs, neutralised in accordance with the SOPs.'

The SOPs contain an explanation for everything under the sun in both war and peacetime. The definitions are clear, concise and precise, as if written by mediaeval scribes destitute of all inspiration. Ready! Aim! Fire! Eliminate enemy personnel with three short bursts. Reload! Discharge! Heel! Fetch! Dive to the right! The assault rifle is effective up to 400 metres, in case of co-ordinated fire by two or more firers up to 800… The SOPs are the finest ency-clopaedia of the insanity of pedantry, SCH in tactical boots.

'Ain't easy bein' alive, going about in the world in this body,' laments Beardo.

A week ago, last time we were on duty, we buried the corpse where it lay. A bullet had ripped up the tendons on his right wrist. They poked out like severed power cords. Another bullet, the one which killed him, hit him below the left breast, near the heart. The blood was partially encrusted there, gelatinous. Above the entry wound, on his camo vest, hung a hunter's pin badge, silver-coloured, slightly rusty. On the pin were two *doubles*, a hunter's hat and an oak twig.

He lay on his back when we found him. Birds had eaten his eyes and the soft parts of his nose and ears. His eyelashes looked monstrous, trimming two empty eye sockets like sunflower petals bordering the pistil. His neck, swollen with decay, was locked by the collar of a camo shirt. I took the vest off him, in spite of the soldiers' superstition that says never to take anything off the dead. He was thickset, with short, Teutonic-blond hair. About twenty-two. A sturdy village lad. The cold had conserved him, stopped further decomposition. Soon he was in his underwear and boots. After that we buried him. Nothing is more real than the human body when it starts to reek.

At home, Mum soaked the vest in cold water, to wash off the blood. The water took on the colour of rotting cherry with streaks of clay, the tub was a brimming blood bath. I left the pin in the drawer as a memento. I wasn't thinking about soldier's superstitions. Everything was happening to me for the first time.

Mum washed and darned the vest. I put it on like a proper front-line fop and went back on duty. Sometimes you think you're invisible in camo, and therefore also indestructible. The better the camouflage pattern, the more invisible you are, and the longer you'll live.

After ten minutes of vigorous digging we struck the corpse. We didn't see any maggots, the soil was too hard and cold for them to do their thing. Only the bacteria of decay were patient and relentless. We wrapped him in a shelter-half and took him to the line. It was one of those specious ceasefires during which a sniper could easily send you to the happy hunting ground.

Between the lines, in a barn full of rotting hay, we met with the Autonomists. We rolled the corpse in on a wheelbarrow. They brought two sacks of flour, ten litres of cooking oil and a sack of sugar. A small fortune. We transacted the exchange, smoked a fag, shared a few words and went our separate ways. In war, when barter is practised, even a dead man has a price.

2.

Miki procured a matchbox of weed. We scrounged together a tenner. Bought a bottle of rot-gut. Some call this rakia powderpiss, because there's a story going round that it's made with soluble powder. That's of no concern to us, what matters is that it hits you in the brains.

In the park, by the primary school, we're smoking the weed, washing it down with rot-gut. Dusk rises like dark dough. The stars are twinkly flakes of bran. The dark matter is made of rye. Above the school entrance there is a placard: *Army of Bosnia and Herzegovina – the guarantor of your survival.* In the deep grass, humanoid statues are randomly arranged for display. All that culture is suffocating. It's like peacetime.

Mama statue is holding a baby in her arms. Baby statue sleeps on the mighty tits that are green with mould. Its head is the size of a football. The weed and the rakia make the world twice as good. They bombard the brain with cluster bombs of rapture. The statues grow turquoise wings and soar to the sky like Wenders's angels. My legs are full of lead. Miki is moving stars with his gaze. He's really good at it. He's rearranging the constellations. We sink into the dumps as if into a black hole. There's also the reeds, when you snap like one.

'Did ya see me bring that star down?'

'Fuck it, let it suffer,' I say to Miki. 'Rock 'n Roll all night!'

'Fuck a fighter that 'asn't been wounded. 'old on a sec, mate, am I right or wot?' Miki slams his fist on the ground, fixing my gaze, his eyes agoggle.

'Right as pie,' I reassure him. 'The dumps and the reeds – brothers.'

Miki sheds tears the size of white small-grain beans. We share the last fag. The rot-gut is as sweet as kiwi juice, and there's still some left. Puff, puff me, puff, puff Miki, right down to the filter. There's always things that piss on your parade. Why not make half-metre fags? You smoke till you become tired, flick the ember off, take a little break then light up again. Absolute bliss: death by smoking. You're going to get killed anyway, lung cancer or no lung cancer, who gives half a fuck?

'I'm off to take a piss,' says Miki. 'Alcohol and weed/making spirits bright/what fun it is to drink and smoke/and piss whilst high as a kite,' he sings.

'Take one for me, too. And see that ya don't step on a mine!' I shout after him.

His gigantic shadow lags behind his body and turns the corner of the schoolhouse. A cuckoo is calling in code understood only by madmen. The rhythm of his elegy is akin to the tick-tocking of a clockwork bomb. Above the park is a road on which cars seldom travel. Their lights illuminate the schoolhouse windows and façade like searchlights in a concentration camp. We're on leave for two more days, it's as though we had two gold ingots in our hands. Nothing else matters: news from the front, or whether or not there's going to be any food and ammunition. The weed and the rakia make the world twice as good. And the future, that syphilitic whore, promises riotous revelries.

The street lamps are out of order. I can't think of a reason why they should work anyway, it's more intimate like this. Only the priority facilities have electricity. And the homes of priority citizens. The darkness swallows us. Chews us up as we dream. It chucks us back up in the morning. Hung-over like wraiths, we set out in pursuit of a refreshing drop of alcohol, fantasising about a dewy pint bottle of Karlovačko beer.

3.

On 20 March 1994, a combined arms artillery/infantry attack commences at 09:50. Dugout 1 has eight wounded. On Hasin Vrh tasty ramsons grows. It tastes like garlic. It lowers the blood pressure. Ramsons is medicinal, it slows down ageing. It makes for excellent salad to accompany a plate of bean stew. On Hasin Vrh, dugouts are made of rocks. They aren't even proper dugouts, more like sangars with very thin roofs. Makeshift weekend cottages for meditation in conditions of imminent danger to life and health. For nature lovers: clean mountain air, organically grown food. UNHCR's reinforced plastic sheeting offering protection from the rain. It filters sunshine, removes the dangerous ultra-violet spectrum. Everything is the result of improvisation. The sky is improvised. Weapon systems, trees, rocks, insects and beasts, too. Around seven dead and thirty-five wounded is another product of improvisation. Only one dale has been lost. In it grows magically scrumptious ramsons. Shells, let off from mortars, whistle through the air like fatwas.

Amir carries me down the country road. I'm wounded in the left foot. In front of us a rifle grenade lands near a group towing a fighter wounded in the spine. His legs drag lifelessly behind him as if they weren't his. We dive onto the forest floor from the road. Fifty metres to the left of us their battle cries ring out. Our line cracked like a china vase. Gone up the devil's mother's fanny. In my Kalashnikov I've got some five or six rounds. Enough to blow my brains out and end the war forever.

Forcing the River

'We're all gonna get killed here, down to the last man,' says Zica.

Rotting pears squish under our boots. In the fruit, sugar turns into alcohol. I've never got drunk on a dry line. The crown of the pear tree, like an old lady, leans over the narrow ginnel we're traversing at double time. The magazines in my tactical vest bounce like Rambo's breasts when he jogs. In daytime this street is covered by an eight-four. It's always safer at night. That's why we're fuckin' running. We are in enfilade along the length of the alley, some fifty metres. The feeling is so intense you can't think, you just rush headlong like a wildebeest.

We are sitting ducks until we reach the sheltering lee of the next house. Once there, we light up, gasping for breath. The wind brings the echoes of gunfire from the canyon, expanding bullets pop as if in a chain reaction. A torn curtain is hanging through the broken window. The TV shelf is covered in dust. The house has been looted. Home appliances fetch good prices. In the rear, a TV set is worth 100–200 marks, depending on the make. Those with flat screens are the best. *Trinitrons*. Like some kind of aliens from Star Trek.

Žile is fascinated by *Trinitrons*. Because the word sounds good. I guess. One time Juso Longcock and I *commandeered* an electric motor from a construction company. We wrapped it up in a humanitarian aid blanket and dragged it for almost twenty kilometres to the village of Gnjilavac. Juso sold it there and went to the nearby town of Kladuša with the money. There are people who like to steal bars of soap, chainsaws, transformer oil from substations, or designer furniture. Others look for gold or hard currency. Žile has a penchant for coffee. Paški for Levi's 501 jeans. Bijeli loves glasses and cutlery. He was a waiter before the war.

I'm lying. On one operation against the Autonomists I stole an Ambassador blanket, still in the original packaging. On the next operation, after I'd taken a pocket watch off an elderly corpse, with a relief of a capercaillie on the lid, I was wounded in the left foot. A piece of shrapnel the size of a marble crushed the first metatarsus, which is attached to the big toe, and lodged itself somewhere in the fleshy part. The pain was unbearable the following few days. I'd bang my fist on the wall, the nurse would come and hit me with a shot of morphine. For the next six hours I'd be in a state of bliss. Next to my bed lay a fighter with a high amputation. He was wont to sing some knicker-dropping turbo-folk number whilst the nurse dressed his wound. From time to time he would complain of phantom pain and an itch in the toes he no longer had. His leg had been cut off above the knee. I screamed when the nurse stuck her tweezers into my wound. She twisted them clockwise, as if to tighten down a bolt. At times I was too embarrassed to scream in front of the amputee, so I'd refrain from complaining about my own pain. The nurse would douse my wound with hydrogen peroxide which ate away the rot and the dead tissue. It foamed like Schweppes. A scab slowly formed on the surface, and the pain subsided. Ever since, the piece of shrapnel in my left foot has forecasted the weather as accurately as any weatherman.

I spent four months walking on crutches, like a run-of-the-mill wounded soldier. Soon the rubber tip on the right crutch wore down, and the crutch made a distinct sound. My dog would recognise the sound of me from a hundred metres away. I called him Humpy Horsie, because he'd started ambling after he survived distemper and had a hump on his back due to his unnatural gait. We lived in that house as refugees. Horsie would happily jump on me, together with a pack of neighbourhood strays. He obviously liked the smell of alcohol, I always came home drunk. There was no way I would ever fall, although I walked on three legs. After the fight with Ramo Puškar, when I hit him over the head with it a few times, the crutch was all bendy like a downhill ski pole. The morning after, my old man straightened it on the wood splitting block with an axe.

It was a joy being wounded. You get cigarettes in hospital, the meals are good and regular. Your friends come to visit you with cans of Skopsko beer. Some of them probably envy you. Girls, too, eye you differently; you're a seasoned warrior now. Tales of your heroism go round, you hog the limelight at piss-ups. You tie your hair into a ponytail with a stocking suspender your friend gave you. Politicians hold you in high esteem. They give you two boxes of Macedonian Partner cigarettes. You give a TV interview. And all that because your girlfriend got married in Germany and it became all the same to you whether or not you died on the next line you were sent to.

* * *

A clump of ash, half the length of a cigarette, falls onto the shiny tip of my boot, polished with lard. The sun is coming down from its zenith to our side of the river. In the hillside neighbourhood of Tećija, a single-storey house hit with incendiary bullets is burning. It's much easier this time round, we move down the main street, lined with houses, no need to run. Like a demarcation line, the Una splits the town in two. We got the shabbier part, with endless factories that *dream and croak in the fog*, and the railway station that phantom trains speed through. Most of us used to live on the other bank of the Una, now out of reach.

'What are we supposed to do on Sokolov Kamen?'

'Nothin', we're goin' to harvest some mushrooms. Caesar mushrooms are the size of an 'andball up there.'

'Fuck Caesar mushrooms,' Žile persists 'how far is that feathery cunt's crag anyway?'

'Round an 'our and an 'alf,' shouts Zgemba.

'It's an op, no two ways about it,' Žile continues 'across the Una, through the mine fields, then attack.'

'Well, are we commandos, or wot?' Zica speaks up.

'Right you are, Zica, in this episode we all die, like on telly.'

* * *

We've passed through our sparse minefield. We're descending a steep canyon. Down below flows the Una, snake-like, green and blue. A group of commandos and a company of trenchies are already on the other side. We're going as a supporting unit, to relieve the commando platoon that broke their line. Before the war this place was an enormous hunting ground. Sokolov Kamen, falcon's bluff, looms high above us. It's a giant block of rock stuck into the foot of Mala Gomila hill. Gravel slides from under our boots and rolls down, drawn by gravity. After fifteen minutes of descent we reach the railway. We pass underneath it through a small underpass. I duck down to dodge a cobweb. The drops of dew caught in it preserve the light of the morning stars. Hari the Kike and Neđo Head of Mutton are dragging the body of a dead commando. Kike gives me about two fistfuls of rounds. We're low on ammo. I've got only one magazine, the one that's already in my rifle. Žile, ever an enthusiast, is going without a gun. Bajrama's Boyo is kitted out like a brave, only his tomahawk has got a rubber head, so he's slinging a bolt-action M-48 over his back. Before the war, Bajrama's Boyo chopped up his front door with a chainsaw when the police came to evict him.

Just before we climbed down the canyon we ran into our brigade commander, down by the Mijić family houses. He swaggered about as if he'd just captured three-quarters of the known universe. Caesar and Napoleon were mere pawns compared to him: the quintessential stuffed peacock. His left hand never let go of his Motorola, whilst he gesticulated lavishly with his right, as if the other person could see him. He told us there was an abundance of weapons and ammunition waiting for us on the other bank. An HQ signals officer gave Zica a Motorola along with brief instructions on how to use it. After that we called all radios Motorola, because that was the first brand we were introduced to.

The corpse Kike and Muttonhead carry is dressed in an American camouflage uniform. The man had come from Croatia, where groups of our people, mostly guest workers from Western Europe, formed units and trained. He had crossed the entire occupied Croatian territory on foot and met his end here.

We cross the river on an improvised raft slapped together out of two lorry tyre inner tubes connected with rope, floored with beech planks. A steel cable is stretched from bank to bank. At our crossing point the river is only twenty metres wide. We go one by one. The Una is low in September. Rocks of tufa, overgrown with reeds, jut out of the water. The bank is rocky, doesn't lend itself to landmines. We climb up to the asphalt road. It is thinly coated with moss. For thirty minutes we climb up the canyon. The climb is almost alpine. Bajrama's Boyo reluctantly discards his rubber-headed tomahawk. Halfway to the plateau we meet the company medic and a fighter who had heart palpitations from fear. Like two jackdaws they're resting on a tree growing out of a crack in the rock.

'Look at that cove, as sallow as a lemon,' Zica says to me.

'The devil's stroked his fore'ead.'

'Done for, poor sod.'

The cardiac patient was completely lost. He stared at us, unable to say anything. His lips were as white as if he'd kissed a vampire.

At the plateau the situation was less than brilliant. A hundred and fifty men were pushed into three dells, like sheep in uniforms. They held a mere three or four hundred square metres of space. Like three coffee cups of territory. Every now and then they were being plastered with cannon. A cannon shell is super fast, immediately after the firing comes the detonation. The officer in command at the plateau was as befuddled as a pigeon that's just shat itself. He was looking at the map, trying to explain something to Zica. Vowels, consonants and spit came out of his mouth at random. Word fragments. Just as we were about to go on recce, a salvo from a multiple rocket launcher crashed onto our positions. Panic was army general. Men dropped their guns and fled down the cliff. Žile took an M-53 machinegun with a long belt from a fleer. He pined for a machinegun like someone pines for a sports car. Being a machine gunner was a matter of prestige. Seventeen trenchies were WIA, some slightly, some severely. We fancied ourselves proper dogs of war, but that bubble burst like a hymen when the rocket launcher opened up. I was overcome by low fever. We took up positions behind hornbeam trees and waited for the infantry assault. I helped Žile by holding the ammunition belt of his five-three. They fired sporadically and randomly at our tight line. Bullets ricocheted and whizzed high up in the air, knocking bits of bark off the trees which landed on my hair. Driven by fear we returned fire, we fired like mad. It looked as though they were putting out probes. River fog was driving down the canyon. Night found us lying behind the trees. None of us had slept, because of the cold, and the rush of the skirmish. In the dark, our eyes were out of combat. Our ears still had a function. We fired at every noise coming from in front of us. Dormice leapt from branch to branch screeching like children. In the morning, Žile announced that his haemorrhoids had flared up. Further defence of that pathetic bridgehead had lost any military significance. The multiple rocket launcher could turn us into martyrs any moment. A slapdash retreat commenced. The strategy of our command was to keep telling us, "They've got no will to fight, we have." Shells have got no will, they're merely full of explosives. Shrapnel kills morale.

A TAM lorry waited for us by the Mijić houses. The radio bleated on about yet another successful operation by the Fifth Corps. The audience were thirsty for territory. We quietly hopped on and sat on the wooden floor. The smell of paraffin, cut with water, forced its way up our nostrils. The lorry revved and trailed a wake of dust. Our faces were tribal masks.

At the Psych Ward

'Year of birth?'

'1969.'

'Height?'

'187.'

'Weight?'

'Around 75 kg.'

'Occupation before the war?'

'Student.'

'Married?'

'No.'

'History of mental illness in the family?'

'No.'

'Army role?'

'Platoon commander.'

'Trenchie or commando?'

'Both.'

'WIA?'

'Yes, once, fragment injury to lower extremities.'

'Which sector?'

'Grmuša–Srbljani Plateau.'

'Addicted to narcotics?'

'No, but I like to drink.'

'Do you take pills?'

'If there's no alcohol, I take what I can get.'

'Nightmares?'

'Sometimes.'

'Do you smoke?'

'I smoke pole, like everyone else here.'

'Describe depression, in visual terms.'

'Grey. Shapeless. Swollen river. Murky sky. Bare trees. Going to a wedding without your cock. No booze.'

'Have you been treated for alcoholism?'

'No, everyone drinks here.'

'What do you mean?'

'I mean, here, in war, what else would people be doing?'

'Do you take marijuana?'

'When there's any for the taking, yes.'

'What is your biggest fear?'

'Chickens, birds, beaks and talons disgust me. That skin over a bird's eyes. I'm scared of all feathery creatures. Even chicks disgust me. If a hen were to give me chase I'd die on the spot.'

'Do you dream of worms?'

'I don't. I dream of slaughtering an obese man in a white shirt. I slice through his chin lump. I stick him in the belly. A dark red ring forms round the wound. He's a civilian. In a fraction of a second, his shirt turns red, like in a film. Then I run away. They chase after me through a gully of some kind. I run down the beck. Hills are all around me, and woods. Branches creak in the wind. Bloodhounds bark. I sweat. I am behind their lines. I have to make my way through their trenches. I worry that I might die from friendly fire as I approach our lines. His children were screaming. The white walls were splashed with blood, like in an abattoir. My conscience troubled me. I felt bad for the man, and he was dead. The walls, freshly whitewashed, were splattered.'

'How many times have you dreamt this dream?'

'Three or four times, I don't remember exactly.'

'Do you read?'

'Well, there's a war on, it's boring, everyone reads.'

'What is the last book you've read?'

'*The Sun Also Rises* by Ernest Hemingway.'

'Was there anything about that book that made an impression on you?'

'The characters were shitfaced all the time.'

'Have you killed anyone?'

'I don't know. I have fired in anger, though. Everything happens so quickly. In an instant. You don't see anything. I may have hit someone, I'm not sure...'

'Do you believe in God?'

'No, but if he does exist, I'm under no obligation to prostrate myself before him.'

'Tell me about an event from the war that's made an impression on you.'

'There have been many.'

'The first thing that comes to mind.'

'Well, one fighter caught a ton-twenty in the thigh. The shell didn't explode. He was lying to the left of me. Mirso was an extremely muscular man. He had just taken a bath. He was smoking a fag. On his right thigh he had an ashtray made out of a luncheon meat tin. I was reading Sartre's *Nausea*. Paperback. The book smelt of mould. We were in a former discount shop, shrapnel had pockmarked lunar sceneries into its façade. We turned the ground floor into a dormitory. It was a three-storey building. Two prefab slabs and one concrete, plus a more-or-less undestroyed roof. A mighty redoubt. We thought we were safe. Along the walls we arranged sofas and mattresses from the nearby houses into L-shapes. To our left was a large shop window, to our right, some thirty metres behind, the river. In front of the window we stacked up Siporex blocks to protect us from shrapnel. They couldn't hit us with their ZiS cannon because of the terrain configuration. With mortars they could though – the shells landed on the roof. It seemed to us we were safe there. At night we kept sentry duty by the river. By day, lookouts observed the river in case the enemy crossed. Who would force a river in broad daylight? It was dangerous at night. And at daybreak, when fog rises. Just as I immersed myself in the book, I heard an explosion. Not too loud. I raised my eyes. I looked at the ceiling. There was a hole there. Greyish dust hovered in the air. Mirso was screaming. A 120 mm shell landed onto his luncheon meat tin ashtray. I picked it up. Held it in my hands. These shells weigh round fifteen kilos. I put it down onto the white ceramic tiles. Its fins had fallen off. Fins are the bits that look like fletching. The tin assumed the shape of the shell's nose, like a mould. Its bloody mask. Without thinking I ripped the t-shirt off my back to use as a tourniquet. Huka found a piece of lath and we tightened up my t-shirt over the wound to stop the bleeding. I put on my camo jacket. The shell had dislocated his leg from his hip. The wound was massive. The bone was sticking out of it. The flesh was minced. It looked like a crushed veal steak. Do you mind if I smoke?'

'Not at all.'

I took three puffs and the cig broke in half.

'What happened then?'

'Huka and I took him to the rear on a stretcher. Two fighters helped us, but I don't remember their faces. At some points we had to run. Shells were falling all along the way. They were targeting us with an eight-four and an anti-aircraft gun. Loaded with expanding bullets. Mirso was heavy. It felt as though I was carrying a celestial body rather than human, as though I had a hot meteor on the stretcher. As we carried him through a neighbourhood, protected from fire, civilians were watching from their doorsteps. I saw scarf-trimmed faces of women contort and bend out of shape with fear. I'd never seen anything like it before, except in frescos.'

'Did the casualty survive?'

'He did. I went with him to the brigade hospital in the van. He asked me to keep his hands warm. He was wrapped in humanitarian aid horse blankets. There was something cadaverous about the scent of his sweat. The waterproof fabric of the stretcher was soaked in blood. I rubbed his hands trying to keep him warm. He was as cold as a berg of ice. We put him in hospital. I never saw him again. I went to a kafana called *Šoferska noć*. Inside, a busty waitress was dancing on the bar. Beads of sweat were breaking on her freckled face. I had Mirso's crusted blood on my chest and under my fingernails. I saw Šmek at the bar. We chased shots of cognac with beer, and were pissed as newts in no time. From the end of the bar, a certain Stranjac, that's what he said his name was, a police inspector, started to praise Fikret Abdić's prudent policies. I remembered how Deba was killed on Murat hill. I walked up to him, chambered a round in my father's Tokarev and shoved the barrel into his mouth. I told him to suck the pistol. He was as meek as a lamb. A policeman snatched the gun from my hand. I took a hand grenade out of my jacket pocket, an M-75, the one with three thousand lead balls in it. The Devil's Testicle. I pulled the pin. People stepped away. I hated the civilian police from the bottom of my soul. A military police patrol walked in. I recognised Sudo – we used to be in the same company. He calmed me down. I replaced the pin and handed the grenade to Sudo. He promised he would return it to me the next morning. The inspector left the scene, together with the policeman who'd snatched my gun. We got back to drinking, now with the municipal mayor. Every time it was his shout, the mayor shouted: 'Allah is the greatest!' I went to the police station to get my gun. The fog was as thick as marijuana smoke in a plastic

bottle. The soldiers' cemetery, Ometaljka, was strewn with wooden
nišan grave markers. They rotted together in the dark, the dead and
their nišans. At the UN container, where the police were quartered,
I ran into the policeman. They are cunts who shirk from frontline
duty and grandstand in front of civilians in the rear. I immediately
socked him right in the gob. He stayed on his feet. He was twice
as strong as me. He punched me and I fell on my back. If it wasn't
for Himzo, his OC, the idiot would've lamped seven bells of shite
out of me. I went to the brigade command HQ to see a friend of
mine, a signalman posted at the phone exchange. In the morning,
other people's voices were humming in my ear. I couldn't control
my own thoughts. My hearing was turned up to the max. I thought
other people could hear my thoughts. I decided to see the brigade
doctor and ask to be referred to a psychiatrist. And I did. My head
is full of dead people, friends and acquaintances. I would often find
myself overwhelmed with feelings of guilt and shame when I met
their parents and relatives. At times it seemed as though I was trying
to explain how come I was alive. When somebody you don't know
gets killed, you're sorry pro-forma. Besides, there is no time for
mourning. A day on leave, in your civvies, can be fantastic if there's
fags and alcohol.'

'What will you do if you survive the war?'

'I'll eat and drink like billy-o. I'll try to live. The prospect of
peace scares me a bit. It's hard to imagine a world without war. That
just sounds like sci-fi to me.'

The fish-faced psychiatrist scribbled a prescription and handed it
to me across his desk. He asked me to tell the next patient to come
in on my way out. I opened the door. A throng of people were in
the waiting room, as if waiting for a giveaway of coffee and fags.
The light was flickering in the bulb. The hallway reeked heavily of
piss and medicine. Hell's hospital. I looked at the paper: Follow-up

in twenty-one days, therapy of pills with a strange name. Twenty-one days of leave! What bloody leave! It's gonna be pure suicide by alcohol and supplemental substances. Living life to the fullest.

'Next!' I said, smiling.

And I started making my way through the crowd towards the light outside.

EPILOGUE

That evening we languished all the endless livelong night at the sentry post by Mujo's stable, peeking through the window at the slick surface of the Una. We were so tired we were seeing enemy boats slicing the slow main stream of the river with their sharp cutwaters. Styx took two hours to recount his own encounter with the psychiatrist. Almost every seasoned fighter I knew had been to the psych ward at least once. It was a lifestyle thing, like Bushido. I purposely polished up some of the rougher bits, without wishing to undermine the authenticity of his story. Styx, whom I'd never asked about his real name and was embarrassed to do so later when we became close, lost the gift of speech when he was wounded in the neck in the autumn of 1994, when we took Radić Hill for the first time.

I'd often visit him when I returned from the front. Once he used his hands to ask me to read him the things I'd written down on sentry by the Una. I produced my notebook, which I always had on me, stared at the logo of the Tourist Office of the town of Bosanska Krupa, and started to read slowly. He stopped me halfway through the text and asked for a piece of paper.

That's not how it was – he wrote.

How was it then? Better or worse? – I added on the page torn from the notebook.

Much nastier – he wrote, and motioned me with his index finger to press on.

He moved his lips and tongue as if he were spelling the words I was saying. He flailed his arms with the passion of a Biblical prophet. I didn't quite know if I was reading to him, or he to me. When he worked himself up, from his throat emerged netherworldly phonemes, sounds from the times when words reflected the primeval nature of things.

A Circular Letter

I am a time bomb. Compressed into living matter. I curse the day I was born. I wait for someone to flick the switch. Button, lever, anything. To nullify the creature thinking in me. To raise the heckles of the consciousness.

When I go back to the frontline I'll shoot cows, horses, sheep, chickens, dogs, grasshoppers, hay. Everything that breathes and slithers. I will shoot the grass and the soil. Let houses burn like candles on birthday cakes. I will shoot the sky above their line, the clouds will ooze the proletariat's colour. I will shoot at my own rear. Let all sides feel the pain.

The fan on the ceiling is turning like an aeroplane propeller. My sweat smells of burnt plastic. There's been a short circuit. Threads of fast-burning nerves have touched. The sky is as stable as the mount of a 12.7 mm anti-aircraft gun. So long as the air doesn't sway. Oxygen, nitrogen, hydrogen, bacteria and air-dwellers. Let the spirits of the air die, and with them a billion frivolous gods. Beer tastes like diesel. Crack, crack, crack, ttziiiing, a sniper is chirping like a robin high up in the crown of a tree. I breathe the resplendent emptiness in full auto mode.

There is no point.

Has there ever been any point?

The burial mounds are stuffed with cadaveric fighters. Festooned with wild herbs. Crocus, iris, dandelion. I live in an enclave. The internationals call it the 'Bihać Pocket'. I live in a pocket. Fast and recklessly.

The *Bofors* fires in bursts. Its calibre is 40 mm. It is used to shoot down aeroplanes from heights of up to 3000 metres. The brass casing of its shells can be used as a vase or an ashtray. Twack, twack – sniper rifle bullets hit the stone retaining wall above the railway. Nice sound, that. A spark here and there. A game of darts with human lives.

Fragments rule the world.

We've broken their line. Steam rises in the midday sun. About thirty of us shout the *Takbir*, sheltered behind a house and a stable. We're driving them away with war cries. A calf moos lying in a thick layer of cool ashes. We split into fire teams. We attack across a green meadow. Grass bends beneath my boots. Releases greenish juice. Soaks the soil. Ants scurry about their devastated homes. Bury their heads in their hands. Repair the damage. Bury their dead. Erect monuments. Sing dirges. Write prose.

I will shoot everything that breathes and slithers.

There is no point. The point is a flaccid condom tossed onto the street after a good shag. Trampled under soldiers' boots.

Droplets of Diazepam spittle quiver on my moustache. I live in an enclave. The official name used on the radio is the County of Bihać. We've got a lot of territory. You couldn't cross it on horseback in four days. A few hundred square kilometres, or perhaps over a thousand. Enough to breathe, and that's nothing to sneer at.

Details rule the world.

I am pissing on the lip of a dale and a fabulous copse. Lovely cyclamen sprout from the forest floor. I seem to hear the flap of wings. A sixty drops five metres below my bollocks. I see the flash. A raster image of chopped off branches, leaves and cyclamen. I run to the house where we're quartered and waiting on stand-by. Inside, men play poker for fags. I can only see their lips move like in a silent film, because I've gone deaf from the blast. What a fool I am. I must stay calm – and that, too, is a trifling matter. Fuck the supreme command of the universe!

The tank is a squeaky monster. It's got many eyes and hands, and ball bearings in its legs.

The latrine mirror reflects my face. It is the face of Buster Keaton.

Calm down. Calm down. Breathe in – breathe out. One, two, three, four… Breathe deeply. Connect your thoughts with safety pins. While here seconds drag on as if in the distorted space-time of a black hole, somewhere out there chronometric time glides calmly like the lazy waters of the Mississippi. Civilians bathe in the Adriatic Sea.

Try to praise the mutilated world.

The tank is a squeaky monster. Eats kids for breakfast.

'The world was much fairer back when Bruce Lee meted out justice,' Zica tells me as we lie in a mucky trench – trenches are mucky by default – waiting for our shell to chalk down a pathetic THE END or FIN.

The plot line's fucked up. It blew up into smithereens like an RPG in a hornbeam forest.

Fractals rule the world.

'You don't know the first thing about life!' Ćipo yells at me 'I've got a woman and two kids! You don't give a fuck, you can stay here for three years at a stretch! Still wet be'ind the ears! I've a family to feed!'

Ćipo was KIA on Ćojluk hill in the summer of 1995. He was laid onto oak planks. Decomposition had spared his face. He had three scratches on his forehead. Wrapped in a winding sheet, he was lowered into the ground. The soil was brownish red and dry. It crumbled between the fingers. Rays of sun were shining into the grave at an angle. Death is not the point at the soldiers' cemetery Ometaljka. That's just hackneyed civilian lingo.

I will shoot all things living and dead. To turn reality into mince.

THE PURSUIT OF WARMTH

Deep in the Rear

'This entire load of bollocks is like a never-ending Woodstock. Only there's no music and there's a lot of dead and wounded. Otherwise fine.'

'Is there nothing besides the war you're able to talk about?' Zu asks me.

Turns out there isn't.

Rain rinses the enormous main room of the café. Leaning on our elbows we look through the window as if through the eye of Polyphemus. We gaze through the rain. A cherry tree, bereft of leaf, looks like the monument in the Jasenovac Memorial Park. Raindrops are creeping down its bark. In the distance before our eyes, hillocks, as like as two eggs, make up a curvy horizon. We fog the glass with our breath. With the pads of our fingers we doodle in the condensed steam. Warm air from an electric fire hits our backs. To our right, on a wooden platform, there is a colour telly. MTV is forever on. Our window into the world outside.

'Shall we have another rakia?'

'What else?' replies Zu.

'Do you see the mites at the bottom of the tumbler? It's the floaters, bits of the barrel, rakia eats it away and it dissolves slowly. They say they put a quince in the barrel to get the rakia to turn yellow.'

'Yup, as yellow as a gold piece,' she confirms.

'See, we can talk about normal stuff, too.'

'We can,' she says. 'This stuff hits you in the brains.'

'Must be at least fifty percent alcohol content.'

'If not more.'

'They add sugar, then boil it.'

'It'll boil our souls.'

'And our brains,' I add.

'In this place, Jesus himself would take to the bottle in two days,' Zu concludes.

MTV is playing Pearl Jam. The song is called 'Alive'. Pure energy radiates from the screen, pumping our blood. Rakia is pumping our blood, too. A shot costs one mark. Ten marks or postal coupons is enough to get proper drunk. And if somebody stands you a round, you're running in the Alcoholympics.

'Samir, two more please.'

'On the house!' Samir shouts from behind the bar.

Well, then, pour one for gramps 'ere,' I shout back, pointing to myself, 'and give us all another round. And turn up the telly!'

'Zu, what do you reckon, what if these aren't floaters? Maybe they are tiny creatures, immortal drunks who live and die in alcohol. And we drink them. For a while they stay in our belly, then in our veins, and finally end up in the sewers. Not a shabby life cycle. From the sewers they make their way into the groundwater, springs, becks, rivers, and into the rakia again. They're completely harmless. They're as dark as bits of faded coal. That's because they're drunk around the clock. I think they're the happiest creatures on the planet and beyond. It's possible they're from another galaxy, one where streams of alcohol are flowing. They probably came to the Earth as stellar spores and colonised home-distilled rakia. In rakia, they have ideal life conditions that remind them of their native planet. They rarely get homesick. They mostly look towards the future. That's how they've survived for millions of years. They don't give a fuck about the past. They're indestructible, like diamonds. But, unlike the precious stones, they are aware of their own existence. There is no hierarchy; they are all equal. They simply enjoy life.'

'What do they think about love?' Zu asks me.

'It's likely that they consider physical love passé. They make love via mental waves. They have no need for touch.'

'Well, they aren't very cool,' says Zu, after she heard me out patiently.

The rain intensifies its assault. Samir is washing up behind the bar. Zu and I are in our regular spot. A pool table is in the middle of the room. Two white cues are tucked under the rail cushions. The cue ball is resting around the middle. MTV is all we have, apart from the rakia, of course. Posters of rock stars hang from the red walls of the café. Jimi Hendrix has got large circles under his eyes. He is wearing a bandana round his forehead. Morrison hides his eyes underneath the glasses. He must be hung over. Everyone says the burden of fame is enormous. Everyone is to be believed. For a moment, The Cult's powerful riffs make us think we're fine. The clock on the wall is accurate. Zu's cheeks are like two ruddy orbs, two candied apples on wooden sticks.

'Have you heard about that calf with a map of Bosnia on his forehead? The map is white, with six golden fleurs-de-lys.'

'Folks say it's an omen, the war will end soon.'

'That's what they said last year, too. Folks say all kinds of things.'

'Well, Zu, as a child I heard that the vein patterns on a bullock's bollocks were actually secret inscriptions in the Arabic language.'

'Wonders and miracles.' She gazes through the window.' 'It's like we live in Macondo.'

Omens are everywhere. Old men sit in the town park and listen to the radionews. They argue about how far the units of the Fifth Corps have advanced. They know everything, as if they've been to the warzone. They believe every word that's coming from the radiobox. And, of course, they have a penchant for embellishing reality.

Omens are everywhere. Messianic messages are woven into the nerves of leaves. All things have their mythical meaning. Stables and stockades are full of calves and lambs with talismans that will save us from evil in this world and lead us into a better one. Autochthonous Bosnian dragons hide in the caves. At night, the feathered serpents of Krajina, endemic to these parts, glide through the air. Whoever finds a feather in the morning has hit the jackpot and just might survive the war.

We sit at Café Ferrari all day long, waiting for something to happen. Nothing out of the ordinary does. Rakia – weed – pills – MTV, sometimes even beer. Beats being on the frontline. Outside, rain-soaked roofs are sinking into the darkness. We observe the change of day and night, like scientists observing cellular division under the microscope. The goings-on under the microscope are accelerated. The rakia, made of plum, is the only constant.

'Long live the roofs of all lands!'

'Long live the fighters of the Fifth Corps, wherever they are!'

'Long live the rain,' Zu supports me.

'Long live the civilians in their cold rooms!'

'Long live the sky, though it's a bit stupid,' I add to the toast.

'Long live MTV!'

'And his good lady wife!' she laughs.

Tremendous thundering interrupts our salvo of toasts. We look through the aquatic window. Bolts of lightning rend the sky and branch out like electrical capillaries. It's just thunder, after all. It's rather hard to tell thunder from the *Volkhov* or *Luna* ground-to-ground missiles or the howitzer shells. You can never be sure which is which. From our ashtray brimming with stubs I pick out one that's still got some tobacco in it. I light it up. The smell of ash and nicotine helps me regain my confidence. Zu finds a stashed fag somewhere in her handbag, a Partner, somewhat squished. She presses the tip against the ember of my faux fag. *It's sad outside, inside it's nice.*

'Shall we fight till the end?' Zu looks me in the eye as if we were toasting.

'We shall never surrender,' I say confidently.

'Never!' she repeats.

The wind changes the course of the rain. It hits our window. Droplets rush down the pane in miniature spirals.

'No pasarán!' I reply, 'as long as we have alcohol.'

A Piece of Shrapnel
the Colour of the Moon

I collect shrapnel. Ever since the war started I've been collecting shrapnel. I put it in plastic medicine bags. These I numerate, and I write down the date and location of discovery, as well as the ordnance type. I arrange them onto bookshelves. The books are carefully stored in *Badel* cognac boxes.

I have in my possession shrapnel of various shape, size and colour. The collection comprises over a thousand pieces. I even have some blood-stained shards, which came from my own body, I removed them with tweezers as soon as they popped out from under the skin. Some pieces fell out of the wounds of themselves. In my back, I've got thousands of tiny shrapnel fragments. I've looked in the mirror, they look like birthmarks. As I was sunbathing on the riverside beach, a girl complimented me on my sexy birthmarks. The doctor said shrapnel that moves underneath the skin or through the muscle, is called mobile shrapnel. Some pieces, however, are immobile – a capsule of fat is formed around the shard, and it stays put. These are the so-called stationary shrapnel fragments.

I would pick them out of trees, the asphalt, out of books (Dostoevsky's *Demons*), out of the ground, out of apples and cherries. I've even found them in flowers. That's not very poetic. Shrapnel is ubiquitous, if the war grinds on, metal will supplant the soil. Tilling the land will become rather difficult. Ploughs will break easily. The planet's core is made out of molten metal anyway.

Asteroids, too, can be made out of metal. Stars are gaseous and liquid, full of dust, their nature is not shrapnelous.

Fragments are often quite jagged and sharp, one should handle them with care – it's easy to get nicked. As they fly through the air they produce different kinds of sounds. Some hiss, others whizz or whistle. The most dangerous are the ones you can't hear at all, it means they're flying towards you. Shrapnel as such isn't found in nature, although almost anything can become shrapnel, even human bone. In a way, its nature is dual, because it can be abstract – it doesn't grow on trees; and concrete – it grows in arms manufacturing facilities, and in its duality it is similar to sunlight, which, as we know, is dual in nature.

And so we have shrapnel in the form of fragments of rock, asphalt, wood, glass and metal. This is the so-called secondary shrapnel. It is produced by the primary shrapnel, which comprises fragments of the casing of a shell, rocket, aeroplane bomb, hand grenade, or pieces of the jacket of an expanding bullet. This means it appears causally. Or in a chain reaction. Both abstract and concrete shrapnel tends to cause mutilation or death. It is therefore best avoided when it flies hot and deadly through the air. Regular-shaped shrapnel fragments are very much a rarity. Only the balls from the M-75 hand grenade are regular in shape, but they are tiny and rarer than specks of gold. And perfectly spherical.

I look through the window. Shells are falling. Mortar, 60 mm, an entrée before the heavier calibres. I go out to hunt shrapnel.

I run across the level crossing by the Lepa Radić monument. Her black torso has been stuck onto a concrete cuboid and placed onto a smaller plinth. Her eyes are marble, monumentally blind. Hard by her grows a black locust tree whose rough bark is a shrapnel collector. Her breasts are riddled with shrapnel. Her torso is marble, too: I've got its secondary shrapnel, fragments of her breasts. She is a national heroine whose best before date passed with the advent of new democracies in the region.

I lie down on the road. I put on light brown leather gloves, similar to those chauffeurs wear. Glass is shattering on the asphalt. Remnants of shop windows are bursting from the blasts. I pick up pieces of glass and put them in the pockets of my camouflage jacket. From around the corner of the doorkeeper's booth I peek into the sawmill yard. They are just shelling the sheet metal smokestacks with a B-1 mountain gun. The sight-setter is obviously having fun. Being a sight-setter must be an unusual hobby, like mine. Large pieces of sheet metal and primary and secondary shrapnel fly in all directions like saucers. Every time the cannon fires over the sawmill, it hits a two-storey house without a façade, whose roof is like a block of Swiss cheese. Reddish clouds of brick and roof tile dust hover in the air. When it falls short the shell ends up in the river, a column of water rises, as well as a centripetal tide wave which washes the two warring riverbanks. It's interesting, like on *It's a Knockout*.

I think shrapnel made of water is impossible. Water shrapnel is like the unicorn, it belongs to the realm of the mythological. I wait for the gunner to become bored with wasting shells, so I can start collecting. Gloomy business, this. You're never done, you can never have enough specimens. Dangerous thing, shrapnel collector's fever.

'How's it goin' mucker?' a civilian shouts from behind a boarded up window.

'Not bad. Room for improvement though.'

'What do you mean to do with all the shrapnel? Build a new Tower of Babel? There's no escaping from here,' the civilian remarks.

'You heard wrong, I'm building a rocket to fly to the Moon.'

'Snapped like a reed,' I hear him mutter to himself.

Can't a man have a hobby without being gossiped about? I don't know where the fascination with shrapnel came from. I lived in

Egypt as a child. I spent four years there. Four years of primary school at the Yugoslav Club in Cairo. In the schoolyard grew a juicy orange tree. My teacher's name was Ljubica Fišer. We pupils went down to the harbour made of white marble to welcome comrade Tito. He sailed in on a ship called Galeb. We waved Egyptian and Yugoslav flags. From his black stretch limousine Tito greeted us, waving a hand in a black leather glove. I didn't see his face.

A Palestinian man often came to our flat. He was a friend of my father's. He wore a piece of bullet on a leather necklace around his neck. He'd fought in a war against the Israelis. I asked him about the pendant once. I didn't understand him completely, I remember only one word: *muerte*, or something like that. Even though I didn't know its exact meaning, there was a ring of anxiety to it. Some words are inscribed into your genes and you can understand them intuitively. Father explained to me later that the Palestinian was talking about death. Maybe that's where my shrapnel mania comes from – many things about our psyche are explained by childhood events.

I've gathered a few sheet metal fragments that were missing from my collection, and set out home. Daylight slowly withdraws to the initial positions. Its nature is dual, just like that of shrapnel. The Una turns blue-green as the light fades. The trout slip under blocks of tufa, on top of which curly-haired reeds sway like the hair of a water fairy. The light disappears from the sight-setters ocular nerve, and his eye is no longer a gun sight.

NOTE

This story failed to meet the criteria of a literary contest for the best sketch or essay on the topic of *How I See My Enemy* organised by the Regional Society "Bosanski Bedem" ("The Bulwark of Bosnia") in the town of Cazin, because the jury found it lacking moral and patriotic motifs, as well as *floating in a sphere of obscurity*. The chairman, a certain Ahmet Hardalović, a literature teacher, pointed out that the author was wanting in national and religious consciousness and lacked a sense of belonging to the Muslim people in these hard times. As for the aesthetic merits of the piece itself, one may complain about the lack of a plot in the usual sense of the word, that is, the lack of events, which, of course, may also be seen as advantageous. However, the jury voiced no opinion. The title, I suppose, was borrowed from a translation of Guillaume Apollinaire's poem "There Is", unless it's an unintentional quote. I recount the story here in its original version, which I obtained for two packets of HBs, to the satisfaction of the author who stressed he wished to remain anonymous, because, as he said, there was nothing special about the desire to be special.

Undertakers' Yarn

'May the war last another hundred years.'

'Why so?'

'Godblessyou me son, I've never shagged so much in me life. They're all willing, to say the least, a lad would need a double-barrel cock to stop all the holes.

'Right as pie.'

'Jus' the other day I was in Kladuša, I picked up a bint for a crystal glass and a tin of Icar beef. We shagged behind a shed. Everyone's happy.'

'I've not seen any in three months, never mind shagged.'

'I 'spect your moves are weak. It's all about the moves. If the moves are strong, you just pick 'er up, like with a shovel, like.'

'Right as pie.'

'Yes, but there were bints for shagging before the war, too. Here's 'ow it was: there was this new waitress started at Mali raj…'

The three of us are sitting on wooden benches under a walnut tree. Green drupes are hanging from the branches. Behind us is a pyramid-roofed two-storey house. Sehu is the one who shags a lot. The one who shags too little is Novad. I'm the one who says *right as pie*. On my way home from the front I decided I'd sleep at their quarters. Novad lights a fag, we follow suit, and he presses on.

'So, anyway, there was a new waitress over at Mali raj.'

He takes a drag, gazes pensively through Sehu.

'Go on man, talk!' says Sehu.

'And so… I order a pint bottle of Karlovačko. Her eyes are fire. Her face cleverish, in fact, a bit too serious for a waitress. I fix her gaze for about thirty seconds. Like I'm penetrating her brain with a power drill. She's not impressed. She's nimble and quick. She pours cognac into tumblers, puts them onto a stainless steel tray and takes them to some idiots sat in the corner. Narrow waist, you could gird it with your fingers. Tiny arse, round and 'ard like a peach. There she is, be'ind the steel-clad bar in the blink of an eye. Proper prima ballerina. I'm throwing glances at 'er, but she doesn't give 'alf a shite.'

'Well, did you fuck 'er?' Sehu asks.

'Steady on, you'll 'ear what 'appened,' says Novad and continues with the story.

'I say, luv, 'ave one on me. So she pours 'erself a bitter and slams it down. She's one mean, badass bint. Those idiots in the corner are arguing about who's 'ad the most beer. I sense aggro, there's electricity in the air. They mention each other's mother. Peaches is ice cold. She just spins round behind the bar, minds her own business, a seasoned waitress. I'm thinkin' to myself – I'll be shaggin' that by the end of this ballad. Like a louse, Novad never gives up.'

'Luv,' I say, 'give me another one, but make it icy. And 'ave one on me.' I touch the bottle – ice cold.

'Cheers, luv!' I quaff down 'alf the bottle. I wipe the foam off me moustache. Me teeth are frozen. She tilts 'er tumbler, shuts 'er eyes and swallows the bitter. She scowls and starts washin' up.

''Ow's business?' I ask Peaches.

'I told you 'is moves were weak,' Sehu whispers in my ear cupping his hand in front of his mouth.

'Not a peep from 'er' – Novad presses on – 'she's washing up staring at the tap.'

'Talkative, are we?'

'Well, somebody's got to be like that round 'ere,' says Peaches.

'Will you be waggin' your chin all day or is something about to happen in this tale of yours?' heckles Sehu. 'Get to the point, godblessyou.'

'Any road, we start to communicate, when all of a sudden the idiots in the corner start to fight. There's blood, and all. We break it up somehow. She brings a first aid kit from behind the bar, bandages the one wot got 'is cunt bloodied. The two *creaturologists* make peace, 'ave one more drink and depart. She takes a seat at the bar and we start drinking. Her name is Silvana. I stroke her hands swollen from cold water. The conversation flows as if we've known each other for yonks. It's the devil's hour, round two in the morning. Prophet Muhammad himself would want to get pissed at two in the morning. I almost fell in luv with her. I must've destroyed two crates of beer.'

'Oh, fuck off, that's gone too far now! A giant couldn't quaff all that down.'

'Right as pie!'

''Old on lads, let me finish the thought,' says Novad. 'So we go to the hotel room. We snog as soon as we get in. I grab her shaved fanny – no clit, no lips. Smooth. I feel an 'ole, like an arsehole.'

Novad folds his index finger into a small knot.

'A tiny fanny!!!' he shows us, with an amazed look on his face. 'Lads, I could 'ardly believe it. I look and I see, it's not in fact an arsehole, it's a fannyhole. I push a finger in, it goes in smoothly. The 'alf-fanny is full of juice. I barely manage to shove in one more. She's squeezin', it's like she's gnawin' at me fingers. Writhin' like a water snake. Me cock's apt to burst. I try to pop it in, but she's as tight as an inner tube. Never seen nothin' like it before. A faux fanny.'

'So, did you fuck 'er?'

'Nah, she sucked me for an hour and a half, I couldn't come.'

71

'Why not shag her up the arse?'

'I couldn't, that's disgusting.'

'Some shagger, you!' Sehu speaks up. 'Just hawk on two fingers, rub it on the arsehole, slide it in slowly. I was expecting shaggery from outer space, three rounds without disengagin'…, not this bollocks.'

'Just me luck,' laments Novad.

'Some blame their luck, others get to fuck,' says Sehu.

'Right as pie.'

'Should've seen my bint from Kladuša. An 'andful of fleshy, wallet-sized clacker, drippings runnin' down 'er thighs. First I licked 'er off. 'Er wallet was as ruddy as, say, a violet,' recounts Sehu.

'Since when are violets ruddy?'

'Roses are red, violets are ruddy, let the man talk, that's poetic license, like,' I get a word in edgeways.

'Then I spread her flaps and 'ad a go with me tongue. Her clit was the size of an 'azelnut. The pubes were getting between my teeth, but I wasn't bothered. She came twice as I ate her out on a wooden stall. Once her cleft was chirked up, I popped it in. She was well-lubed and I slipped in conkers-deep with ease. I was pullin' 'er 'air with one 'and, kneadin' her soft tits with the other. I flipped 'er on 'er belly, slipped it into the wallet from behind. I humped for about twenty minutes, diddlin' 'er clit. "Ohh, this is good," she moaned, impaled on my cock. I spunked on 'er wobbly arse cheeks. We took a short break, just enough to share a fag, and then fucked once more. Now, that was a proper wartime shag. No thinkin', nothin' but fanny in yer 'ead. I was as 'appy as Bruce Lee when 'e does the bad guys over.'

'Right as pie!'

The night lowered its long tentacles into the crown of the walnut tree, like in a fairy tale. Words wore out with all the use. Novad produced a flask of home-distilled rakia. It went from mouth to mouth.

We chain-smoked. We forgot about the sex talk, and each stared at his own ideal point in time and space. A cold summer breeze came in from the forest that surrounded us.

'I shagged a lot before the war, there was all these gang-bangs. Slags are women, too.' Novad tries to justify himself.

'Pass the flask, and shut yer gob.'

'When's the 'orse cart comin'?' asks Sehu, whose real name is Huse.

'Round 11:30.'

Sehu glances at his watch with fluorescent hands and Roman numerals.

'They said five bodies.'

'The shelves are clean, we'll put them on the shelves till mornin'. It's warm though, they should be buried as soon as possible. Give us a hand tomorrow?' Sehu asks me.

'Sure.'

The invisible heartbeat of the night is beating in my neck veins. Sehu and Novad are outside waiting for the cart. I walk into the mortuary. The shelves are covered with white sheets. The wooden floor has been scrubbed, not a speck of blood on it. The plaster that peeled off the ceiling rustles underboot. In the corner, behind the door, three shovels are leaning against the wall. Their handles, slick with frequent use, sheen in the half-dark. Early in the morning we will go to Ometaljka, in silence. Drops of dew will cleave to our trouser legs as we walk through the wild grass ripping up cobwebs. The strong smell of churned soil and sliced up roots will cancel out the perfumes of pollen and the smell of the tall pines opposite. The shovels will swiftly finish their work.

Full Auto

1. He was sitting in dugout 6, to the left of the water reservoir.
   a) It was in the area of Padež hill.
   b) December had brought a dry winter.
   c) Frost-encrusted leaves rustled underboot.
2. In his left hand he was holding an automatic assault rifle by the hand guard.
3. He rested the under-folding stock on his stomach.
4. With the fingers of his right hand he pulled the cocking handle.
5. The extractor extracted the round from the magazine.
6. He saw the brass casing and the bronze-coloured bullet at the mouth of the barrel.
7. He released the handle and the round was chambered.
   a) He was afraid to die.
   b) The feeling passed quickly.
8. He went out into the communication trench which was frozen and impassable.
9. He briefly peeked over the breastwork.
10. Down below was their line, concealed by a thick stand of trees.
11. He set the fire selector to full auto.
12. He leaned a little, lifted the gun above his head.
13. He rested the barrel onto the top log of the breastwork.
    a) Carved in the beech bark was: "Hedgehog porked a stork".
    b) The Army of Bosnia and Herzegovina coat of arms.
    c) Skull and crosscocks.
14. His brain was terribly empty.

a) He yelled: "St Sava is a faggot! I piss on your cross!"

b) In the process, he was shivering with fear and fury.

c) He was clenching his teeth.

d) His lips were shaking.

e) As if before a first kiss.

15. He fired short bursts.

16. After some twenty seconds he spent the whole magazine.

a) His lips and throat were dry.

b) Like papyrus.

17. The barrel of the rifle was hot, and shiny from gun oil.

18. He lit up a fag from the half-empty packet, his daily ration he'd received that morning.

19. The smell of leaf and gunpowder filled his nostrils.

20. That was a daily ritual.

21. From below, they started firing furiously, as if offended.

22. He crouched in the communication trench looking at the bottom of a mess tin.

a) He thought: … a slice of Feta cheese slice of tomato half a fistful of salt… and rakia from a glass samovar… the smell of twat juice on the fingers… hundred and twenty bullets, two hand grenades, let them come, if I diiiie, I'll goooo with noooo regrets… in cowboy films, they all make peace after a brawl… frog legs are tasty… four days till relief.. I've not clipped my fingernails… it's cold…

23. It was raining rifle grenades.

24. Expanding bullets gave rise to a paranoid sense that the enemy was near.

25. He entered the dugout.

26. It was ill-roofed.

27. Here and there, rays of sun full of swaying specks of dust penetrated the plastic UNHCR window sheeting.

28. A comrade-in-arms was whittling a Kalashnikov for his kid.
29. Another was asleep on a stone they couldn't pull out of the ground.
    a) The body of the sleeper was foetus-shaped. Spit dribbled down his cheek.
    b) It was his first time on the line with them.
30. They'd covered the stone with straw and humanitarian aid blankets.
31. The rifle grenades were getting caught in the branches and exploding in the air.
    a) An interesting spectacle for a wartime photographer.
32. Fire from both sides slowly subsided.
33. He returned to the communication trench.
34. It was around half past four in the afternoon.
35. The time when feigned attacks usually stopped.
    a) That was a daily ritual.
36. He was sweating, although it was cold.
37. He took his helmet off, laid it onto the breastwork.
38. The cold breeze felt good on his sweaty head.
    a) His hair was stiff with sweat.
39. He was thinking about what was for lunch.
    a) Beans.
    b) Rice.
40. It was all the same to him.
41. If there was meat in the food, he knew he'd be going on an op.
    a) That was an occasional ritual.
42. He took loose ammo from his right trouser pocket.
43. He patiently loaded the empty magazine of his automatic assault rifle.
44. It had been fifteen minutes since the shooting had died down.
    a) The birds were mum.

b) A perfect melody of silence.

45. Dusk was descending like a brocade curtain at the end of a play.
    a) Clots of black, those minions of night, overran the cracks of white between the dense trees.

46. The dusky sky he was looking at through the dark branches was red.

47. Down below, far behind enemy lines, the Una flowed quiet and awfully blue.

48. Stars were peeking out of their shelters.

49. The reign of the wintry Sun was over.

50. That was a daily ritual.

51. In his dugout, the men were starting a fire.
    a) The toothed wheel of a plastic lighter scraped the top of the flint stick.
    b) Sparks, then greenish-blue flame.

52. He heard them talk about whether or not they would be relieved soon.

53. In the trench in front of the neighbouring dugout somebody was smoking.
    a) His gaze followed the ember.
    b) A few dark circles popped in front of his eyes.
    c) Clots of black were swarming round his heavy head.

54. He was going to be sick.

55. Saliva was pooling in his mouth.

56. He threw up yellowish liquid, splashing his boots.
    a) His head was thundering like the inside of a drum.
    b) His boots reeked of hydrochloric acid.

57. He cleared his throat and spat out stomach mucus along with the odd bit of undigested food.

58. He wiped his mouth and cheeks with the sleeve of his grease-stained jacket.

59. He lit up.
   a) Like Clint Eastwood.
   b) Or Lee Marvin.

Addendum. Stardate 25627.2 Captain Picard's Log:

60. He rubbed ash onto his face and hair.
   a) Lowered his balaclava to just above his eyes.
61. Night-like, he stealthed through the enemy lines.
62. He swam across the river, knife in teeth.
   a) The water smelt of waterweeds.
   b) He swam soundlessly, like a woman.
63. He traversed a minefield, as confident as Jesus walking on water.
64. He reached the tank.
65. It was exceptionally well dug-in.
66. Its long barrel protruded over the sandbag parapet of the gun pit.
67. The crew were sleeping in a pillbox.
   a) Tins of Greek milk and oxidised tank casings were strewn
      all around.
   b) Frozen turd piles were covered with torn up book pages.
68. He climbed onto the sandbags.
69. He hugged the barrel.
70. He bent it earthwards.
71. The barrel became a trunk.
72. The tank turned into a circus elephant.
   a) It pranced up with a mighty roar.
73. He'd done a proper wonder, worked a proper miracle.
74. Hallelujah, hallelujah, went the choir in the trees.
75. I think this is how it happened.

* * *

Osman, nicknamed Jap, was killed in the trench in front of dugout 5 on Padež hill, on 17 November 1994. That trench was known as the sacrificial trench. Before the war he was a literature student in Zagreb. A Bofors shell chopped both his legs off above the knee. The throat of the chimney on the roof of the dugout was slit. As we carried Jap to the command post we were trying to stop the bleeding. He breathed his last just as we were going down the slope wading through layers of rotting leaves. In the commotion somebody gave me his rucksack.

An hour later, out of sheer curiosity, I went through the rucksack. Inside I found this story, written in pencil on white serviettes. I barely managed to decipher some words as the graphite traces on the paper had faded with time. The company morale officer returned the rucksack with the rest of his belongings to his parents. I kept the story hoping it would be published someday.

I put my nose to the window pane. We'd been at the barracks for three days now, waiting for the alert to be called off. Outside it was snowing cats and dogs, flakes the size of a cat's head. I was pacing across the wooden floor of a hut. The boards were bending and squeaking under my shiny boots. The whole hut smelt of rotten chipboard. I'd read the story out loud. After the performance I lit up. In the corner, Red Dog was feeding bits of chipboard to the tin stove. The rest of our platoon were out eating lunch, while some deserted to the village of Pištaline. There were four or five kafanas there that were open 0–24.

'Mucker, how do you like the story?' I ask Red Dog.

'It's good, though I didn't quite get everything… It's passable. The only thing I didn't like is the bit with the elephant. Fuck, that's fantasy. You know that can't be. If it were more realistic it would probably be better overall. But the man had a lot of imagination, I've got to give him that. He's snuffed it any road. He was a good fighter,' Red Dog wraps up his oral review.

'Bad job 'e got killed, 'e was talented, 'e could've gone on to become a good writer,' I say to Red Dog.

'He didn't look after himself. There've been lots of deaths recently. Shame. He's got this one sentence he keeps repeating, "It's a daily ritual". Or something like that. Death, fuck his whore of a mother, is a daily ritual.'

'"That was a daily ritual", word for word,' I pull Jap's sentence out of my memory.

'Never mind,' says Red Dog – the message is the same.

Red Dog reaches under his jumper and produces a packet of Gales from his shirt pocket. He gazes at the foggy window through which polka dots of snow can be made out.

'Fancy one?'

We light up, like in Jap's story.

'Clint Eastwood up his arse,' says Red Dog.

And we stare long at the fire. In silence.

Tits-Up

1.

We are retreating from Radić Hill. A vast mass of fighters from all
brigades funnels down from the lines onto the asphalt road going
through the villages of Veliki Radić and Mali Radić. On the slopes
on Mt Grmeč, someone is lighting the way with a pocket torch as
we descend through the forest. A column forms on the road stretching for kilometres. Thousands of stinking male bodies, armed and
kitted out, in unnatural silence. I've never seen so many fighters in
one place. Horse-drawn carts laden with ration tins, field kitchens,
heavy mortars, water tanks and the spoils of war.

The retreat started a little before dusk. Nagging November rain
has been falling all day. Cabbage rain, they call it here. It's as though
it's been seeping for months now. The humidity it brings gets into
your bones, your heart, your brain. It turns the sodden soil into
slimy mud. Kills shrapnel-riven trees. Washes the colour out of the
asphalt. Sends hordes of greasy clouds to capture the sun. Gets into
your eyes, down your collar, soaks your uniform, boots, weapons.
Blends all the smells together into one musty lachrymator. The
sound of it is as annoying as the shits. It transforms pastel-coloured
leaves into forest fertiliser. An aura of sweaty fog is rising off the
horses' croups. Steam jets forth from their nostrils, and condenses
into cloudy drops on their thick manes. Clouds of fog billow just

above the crowns of the trees. Shod hooves click and clock on the undercut road. The horizon isn't murky and leaden, it is painted with divine faeces.

'Giddyyyyy uuuuup!'

The lash cracks above the horses' croups.

Voices blend.

'Fuck the state and his good lady wife!'

'We'll never return to Krupa.'

'It's the command's fault.'

Šero Hadžipašić is carrying chains for tractor tyres. He looks like Robert de Niro in *The Mission*.

Jasko is hauling three bags of flour wrapped in a piece of lorry tarp. He stops after a hundred metres. Curses. He unloads his wheelbarrow on the side of the road. He kneels. With vigorous strokes of his pocketknife he stabs the paper sacks, rips them open like slaughtered lambs. He pours the flour into the mud.

'You won't be eating this, Chetnik cunts!'

The rain makes dough in the primordial mud from which tufts of grass jut out.

'I'll get you 'ome, if it costs me my life!' Šero hisses through clenched teeth.

We pass through Veliki Radić. By the fountain, which sprays water uncontrollably every which way, our brigade cook is sitting on a classroom chair, crying. He is wearing a helmet. His grown man-face is made grotesque and infantile by the tears he's shedding. And by his lisp.

'Woff going to happen wiv uff now? We're done for!' he sobs.

Houses have been burning since daybreak. Some are already reduced to smouldering remnants. Those that were spared this morning are flaming right now, blazing our path. Heat lashes at my face as I skirt a shed just by the edge of the road. Also ablaze is the primary school in which we slept one night. Early in the morning, as we were on the frontline preparing to attack, their sappers cleared the forest on the slopes of Grmeč, brought ZiS guns and Malyutkas. They targeted our deep rear. Destroyed our Com Centre TAM lorry. Hit the only APC we had available, as well as the brigade command post.

We didn't have the manpower to cover the vast territory we'd captured. In places, gaps of no man's land between our units stretched for kilometres. It was impossible to carry out the planned push towards the town because they were now plastering us from all kinds of weapons. A trenchie was killed by a sniper as he shat behind a Siporex block stable. He was hit in the left ear with an expanding bullet. You could fit a hand coffee grinder in the exit wound. Nobody counted the wounded. At dusk we managed to pull out from the line. We met the battalion commander by the remnants of the APC. He told us about plan B: the retreat. Plan A involved our victorious descent into the town.

In the Com Centre lorry I lost a pair of Levi's Hafura gave me, a few crystal glasses and a set of cobalt blue china. I'd packed all that booty into a transport bag. I'd never had too much luck with plunder.

Pađen joined the loose column of the second company, the chainsaw still on his back. Baldie and Hafura requisitioned an industrial mower. Hafura, who has convalesced from his blast injuries, is steering. Baldie is his co-pilot, sitting on the machine's blades.

'If it isn't worth two grand in Jezerski it isn't worth a button!' Hafura says to Baldie.

We turn and take the macadam road for the village of Grmuša. We sink into the realm of mud.

'See ya at the barracks!' I greet the motorised duo and leave them behind.

The mower, bogged down in the mud, revs like a Singer sewing machine. Merva, Faćo and I battle the mucky foe. The visibility is three to four metres.

'Faćo, give us a fag!' I ponce off.

'Merva, fancy one?' Faćo asks.

We cup the cigs with our hands. Rainwater drips down from the branches, massive drops bombard our heads. We're walking with a group of fighters from the 503 Brigade. They know the area, it's their sector of operations.

''Ere comes a cart!' shouts Faćo.

'Lads, got any room up there?' he asks the artillerists riding on the cart.

'Yeah, if you're a mortar.'

The artillerists are sitting on mortars, wrapped in shelter-halfs. They overtake us slowly. They are followed by an army green van with its headlights off. The gloomy mugs of the men inside can barely be made out through the dancing wipers. We stand on the sides, in two rows, as the van passes by. Faćo turns his head away towards the forest and spits heartily.

'Cunts!'

'When you're a commando, you're less than human,' Merva winds him up.

The cusses dissolve in the rain. We're soaked. We enter a forest tunnel. We turn into men of mud and deluge. The guns slung over our shoulders are the only difference between us and the typhus patients from the film *Battle of Neretva*. The enemy is the same.

2.

It was bedlam in Grmuša. The units were shuffled up like decks of cards for rummy. No Jokers. Some idiots sang ululating rustic songs by the camp fire, which they doused with motor oil. The flames shot up a metre or two in the air – a perfect target for enemy guns. The shitwits barely finished a song when ZiS cannon started to bash us.

Merva hid in the Orthodox church. Faćo and I into a house housing our brigade's improvised command office. With his back towards us, a bloke is sitting in an armchair at the other end of the room. Only his blond hair juts over the plush headrest. I'm talking to Pendžo, the brigade phone op. The bloke tells me to stop the conversation. Zero shite given. Faćo is shouting, happy to be inside in the warm. Pendžo whispers in my ear that a lorry will soon come to pick up our respective units.

'You two, out!' the bloke tells us. He's an HQ officer.

I chamber a round in my Kalashnikov.

'Well, go on then, chuck us out yourself!' I reply.

'I'll drop a frag!' screams Faćo.

'See ya in civvies!' I shout to the little commissioned cunt as I hold the door knob. 'Pen-pushing twat!'

We take it down a notch and get out into a hail of shells, because if we stay inside heads could roll. Faćo stays under the eaves of the command house. I run over to the neighbouring one.

'Let 'em blast me, I don't even wanna hide!' Faćo talks to the subsiding rain.

With great difficulty, I open a door blocked from the inside with a chair. Inside, men are sleeping on the floor and in beds. A wax candle is burning on the table in the middle of the room. I walk into a miraculously empty room. I crawl under a massive duvet in full battle gear. Now they can shell all they want. Through the window I see by the explosion flashes that the barrage is lifting. I'm afraid to fall asleep, because the lorry could leave for Jezerski without me. I take a half-hour kip. The ZiSes fall silent. I hear clamour and the sound of a lorry engine. I take my rifle, open a window and hop out.

In front of the Orthodox church the driver is revving up the engine. Faćo, Pađen, Merva, and others from the second company are standing in front of the lorry. We hop onto the tarpaulin-covered back of the truck. About fifty of us fit inside for that first trip to the barracks. All along the way we hold onto the steel construction that holds up the tarp. We swing like sides of beef on hooks in a fridge car. After an hour and a half we arrive at the barracks. When we set out for Radić Hill it was nine of us in the unit. We're down to six now. Simple maths. The taking of Golo brdo hill cost us one dead, two out of combat. At the company HQ I took my boots off, after two weeks. My feet were two wounds.

'Now, look what 'e's done to 'is feet! Can't imagine what you'd do to mine!' Fudo Mrga, our company warehouse op, teases me.

Mrga brews us some coffee in an electric cooker. A cup of pure bliss combined with cigs at one a.m. Faćo puts on a pair of slippers and his swim briefs and goes to the bathroom for a cold shower. He's been wounded three times and doesn't give a flying fuck about the common cold. Mrga has also been fucked three or four times. Merva and Pađen are unspoilt. Hafura and Baldie are out there riding their mower. I'm so happy I'm alive I don't even think about our wounded and dead. Tomorrow I'm going home on leave, and that is a magical ceremony. The moment I leave the barracks grounds I will become a new man, at least until next time something goes tits-up. Something quite small, like the shrapnel wound on the cheek of the late Izet Grzić.

Kaleidoscope of Memory

At birth, on 14 April 1970, I weighed 3800 g. I was 42 cm long. I'm an April child. As we all know, April is the month of the dead. In August that year, Hendrix died. I would learn that factoid sixteen years after I came into the world. It is now time to delve into my childhood as if into a refreshingly cold greenhole in the Una.

I liked the cosmic sounds of Jimi's guitar. I bought my first cassette tape at the department store. It was an excellent compilation tape. The department store is a Cyclopic cube, cast in concrete at the side of the high street by the hands of our Heroes of Labour. It is clad in dark blue steel plating. I would come to discover that during the first days of the war when it was set alight and I watched the cladding peel off, the cube under the flames was like the cellophane wrapper of a cigarette packet when you singe it with a lighter.

How many words does it take to describe your own life? Twenty thousand? Or fifty thousand, enough for a decent novel? I'm not interested in my childhood. There may be a flashback or two, though. That period of life looks quaint in old black-and-white photographs, but mine have gone up in flames. I no longer possess a childhood. It possesses me. I am a grown man; the skin on the back of my hands is wizening and turning rough. But it matters not, Solea cream is a proper unguent! I unwind after the fourth pint. My memory reaches optimal operating temperature for vaporising watery memories.

Why should anyone give half a fuck about the fact that I've been born? Happens to everyone. We don't come from the conveyor belt, but from the darkness of the uterus, we emerge headfirst and dive right into the bag of dicks that is reality, like a shell fired from a 120 mm mortar. They don't call these shells "babies" for nothing.

If we return to the real here and now, things become dangerous. We are on a hillock named Joja. I'd like to surname it Satan's Tit. Strategically significant strongpoint, hairy sector. We languish in the front dugout. We've got one Gales cigarette, and we're trying to figure out how to split it and who smokes first. The logo stretches from the filter towards the tip, in block letters, G-a-l-e-s, the final "s" reaching the middle of the cigarette. Elvis and I are making psychological preparations for smoking. The third bloke is on admin sanction, his tour extended for evading duty. He doesn't smoke and isn't from our company.

'Drag till ya gets to the letters and pass on,' says the sanctionee.

His name could've been Enes. His suggestion is good. It's quiet outside, razor-cold. No shooting. Below us a wood, a meadow, a beck, a road, a clearing, and their hill, named Osmača. They've dug in a tank up there, which often puts us in a right fucking pickle. There I cut off wartime reality and continue with my remembrance.

I want to give up on the flashback, because I can't remember anything important. Wait, year one, *Marija Bursać Primary School* ... in Tripoli, Libya. I am six years old. Sitting next to a girl who has chicken-pox. I put my bag between us as a barrier, so I wouldn't catch the disease. Chicken-pox never overran my child body.

My hair was wheat yellow. Straight and shoulder-length. Pageboy cut. I was wearing dress trousers. A little striped jacket and a sailor collar over it. My Adidas football boots were jutting out from under the desk. My eyes were as green as the young leaves of the grapevine cladding Nan's house, built with blocks of tufa from the Una. I look through the kaleidoscope of memory. On the second day of war, Nan's house was turned to ashes.

While I was stuck in my memory, darkness fell and loomed over Joja Hill like a murder of crows. A scops owl emitted its call in regular intervals, with metronomic precision. I left Elvis & Enes and went to my dugout in Biljevine. Slept for two hours. Spent two on sentry. Fired a five-three. Threw a homemade hand grenade with a fuse cord. Nevzet "Blondie" Sivić was on the frontline for the first time. As timid as a hare. He woke me up and told me they were sneaking up to our trenches. That's when I threw the fuse cord bomb. It boomed like a 60 mm shell. Leaves fell off the trees from the blast. I blessed their positions with a machinegun, to help Blondie cure the jitters of his first wartime experience.

We're sleeping on horse blankets on top of beds made of hornbeam branches. The soil is dry and the walls of the dugout are crumbling. To the left and the right of the dugout run the two prongs of the communication trench, each ten metres in length. We're decently dug in. Below us runs a beck called Vodomut. So, it's sleeping (there is no such thing as dreams) plus sentry times fifteen sunrises. In war, there are quiet days, too. War isn't just shooting all the time. The important thing is to pass the time till leave without sustaining casualties. In idling, the war machine pumps the blood into the muscles of the high command and the fancy of the civilians. The fear subsides and war becomes part of your body, like an inflamed appendix.

UNDERGROUND HOTEL

I crawled into that dugout on all fours. As if into a wolves' den. It was a freshly dug out dugout. This line was formed on a clearing. The earth had been scorched during a previous operation. On the first night we took a collective kip. No sentry. I dreamt of the Yugoslav

People's Army Orao aeroplanes machine-gunning and bombing us. They had purple five-pointed stars on their wings. The pilots had soft blue eyes, happy and blinking. The engines spouted milky jets that dragged on behind them like umbilical cords.

'Don't be afraid. Won't hurt. Be over in a bit,' said the celestial surgeons waving to us with their leather-gloved fingers.

I was scared stiff. The planes dropped of themselves, crashing down like mortally struck pheasants. The star-studded wings spiralled down towards me. The milky jets dissolved, taking on the colour of curdled blood.

I woke up from the nightmare. Loose blackish soil seeps into my eyes from the dugout ceiling. I was sick to my cock of trenchie life. Company commander gave me two days of leave on account of previous meritorious service. Psychiatrist gave me seven days of med leave. So I spent only one night in the dugout that resembled a caveman's brow. I felt like Tutankhamun in it, only I was no man's idol.

THE PHOTOGRAPH

Now I weigh 70,000 g. I was 180 cm tall last time I was measured, when I served in the Yugoslav People's Army. My eyes have turned darker, probably from alcohol. Juicy, Kosa, Ani and I are standing in front of Café Ferrari. Hari Palić took the picture. It's a colour photo. On my humanitarian aid zip-up boots there are traces of dried mud. We've just returned from the sector facing the Autonomists. Warm October wind is whistling. Ani and I have ponytails. His hair is dark, mine is fair. Juicy is donning a beret made from a camo shelter-half. It's got the Bosnian coat of arms patch stitched to it. Omer Kosa is wearing a blue windbreaker. He and Juicy are sitting on the low beer garden wall. Ani and I are standing to the side. Behind us are red plastic chairs and round white tables. Far in the background is the window reinforced with electrical tape lest the pane shatter from the blasts of long-range shells.

The image is cold and objective. An embalmed section of the wartime. I assume we'll live forever on that piece of plastic-coated paper. But, before we ride into immortality wearing the invulnerable faces of dead men, we ride into Café Ferrari for an alcohol rhapsody.

From Dusk till Dawn

Ramo Puškar threw a hand grenade onto a green stretching behind a row of wooden huts lining a dead-end alley. It detonated near the kafana Rogovi. The frogs in the greenish puddles ribbitted happily on as if nothing had happened. By the fountain we quenched our thirst with rakia and Skopsko beer. Where the water jet ought to have been, evergreen bushes sprouted forth. The dishevelled branches of the bushes resembled the hair of young refugees just awakened.

The concrete fountain had two cascading bowls. We were sitting on the lower level: Ani, Sudo Mophead, Dado Squaw and me. We'd been chugging alone for an hour now, because the female part of the company had gone to bed. A warm midnight wind murmured in the crown of a forked birch tree whose heavy boughs arched over our long-haired heads. The blast of the explosion caused a momentary gust of artificial wind. Plastic bags filled with the hot air soared skywards to the clusters of pygmy stars.

I poured home-distilled rakia into a beer can. I spilt some on my fingers and rubbed it around like hand lotion. I stuck a Partner cigarette between my lips. In my left hand I held the beer can very close to my face. With the other hand I struck the plastic lighter and brought it up to the tip of the cigarette. For a moment, the combustion of the gas illuminated our faces twisted with alcohol. A flame the length of a pan-sized grayling burst forth from the can. My eyelashes were burnt, together with a lock of hair that fell out of my ponytail tied with a red hairband. My hands caught fire. I put it out by slapping my thighs. The charred protein from the hairs smelt of sulphur.

We'd bought the rakia from a man who was the proprietor of two monikers: Duša – Soul – and Grbin. He had virtually no torso. His legs sprouted straight from his neck. His crumpled up face was dominated by a black moustache reminiscent of iron timber cramps. We often bought from him. He'd never fucked us over before. But this time it was night. Sudo and I couldn't see whether white bits were floating in the glass bottle. Hari Kljaja once told me this powderpiss could give you a crooked mouth.

'Duša is a war profiteer!' yelled Sudo.

'What an absolute turd of a man!'

'The universe is watching us,' said Ani.

My hands were tingling. There was no pain, the rot-gut is a powerful anaesthetic. Duša didn't deserve his soulful moniker. His rakia was soulless. The nickname Grbin – Hunchbackson – fitted him better. He was a cephalopod in human form.

Five cunting civilian policemen turned up.

They thought we'd thrown the hand grenade.

They arrested the three of them, and let me go because I was walking on crutches.

'Invalid, you can go 'ome,' said an idiot in uniform.

They handcuffed Sudo and Ani.

Squaw walked behind them.

They walked in line towards the police station, fifty metres from the fountain.

After a few minutes I decided to go to the police station myself.

I walked along a stream that ran through the town. A thin film of water glided down the grass-grown bottom of the concrete stream bed, carrying faeces into the river Mutnica. Varicoloured bits of glass, scattered in the water weeds, twinkled as they absorbed the photons emitted by celestial bodies.

In front of the police station shone a large reflector light crowned with a halo of flies.

Near the entrance a grey VW Golf Mk2 was parked by the entrance.

A moustachioed guard let me in.

Squaw told me Ani and Sudo had escaped.

I headed towards the exit, pressing the linoleum flooring with the tips of my crutches.

Mr Moustache stopped me and told me I was under arrest.

'Who's under arrest? Go fuck your Autonomist spawn!'

I stepped outside. I discarded my crutches, balancing on my good leg like a stunned crane. I dropped my faux Levi's kecks and my pants to my knees.

I grabbed my cock and balls.

'These bollocks defended Hasin Vrh!'

I cursed his dead children, the graves and headstones of his fathers, aborted embryos, his filthy Autonomist scran...

Squaw came out with two policemen.

Hopping on one foot and still screaming, I went over to the guard's booth.

I swung my right forearm and broke the window.

The gash below my elbow gaped like Mick Jagger's mouth during a chorus.

The moustachioed guard hung his head, everyone was silent.

Squaw asked for bandage to dress my wound.

I sat on the Golf's bonnet.

Barely managed to pull up my trousers.

Somebody brought the bandage and Squaw saw to my wound.

Then a policeman in a baseball cap appeared.

He took a small black rifle off his shoulder.

Its magazine contained twenty 7.62 mm rounds.

He set it to full auto.

'Go on, repeat what you just said! Motherfucker, I've been wounded five times fighting the Autonomists! Go on, tell me I'm one!'

I knew if I said half a word the man would staple me through with a burst.

I kept mum, staring at the tarmac in front of my feet.

He had bigger balls.

This emboldened him, and he cursed a blue streak at me.

I was lucky to be wounded, otherwise they would've kicked seven shades of shite out of me.

The military police, whose garish yellow HQ building was near the police house, took us on.

They put us into the custody suite.

There, the re-arrested Ani and Sudo were resting on army beds.

The walls were carved with the names of the prisoners, erect cocks with hairy balls, hearts shot through with arrows, mosques in neat perspective, snakes coiled around daggers, erotic verse, crescents and stars, initials in a shaky hand.

They gave us gelatinous macaroni with what they purported was meat.

MP Sajo Velagin took me to town hospital in a Mercedes, the other three were released.

At the ER a short-haired, blue-eyed nurse checked my wound and re-dressed it. Her sympathies for refugees fit in the following two sentences:

"Some fighters, you lads from Krupa, you just drink and trash bars. Why not liberate your own town and cause aggro there?"

They planted me in a wheelchair and rolled me into a room.

I couldn't walk on my crutches, the wound was exactly where the plastic pads met the forearm.

The surgery was postponed till I sobered up. Anaesthetics and alcohol don't mix well.

I stayed up all night, holding my gashed arm up in the air to stop the bleeding.

In the morning, a surgeon gave me local anaesthesia under the bright lights in the operating room.

The content of the syringe pleasantly spread round my tissue like miraculously icy water.

He poked about inside the wound with his forefinger looking for shards of glass.

He zig-zagged in a long rubber strip which he called a Penrose.

He closed the wound with seven sutures.

The Penrose poked out of one end, dripping with yellowish pus.

For forty-eight hours I languished in hospital.

Fresh casualties were steadily streaming in from the frontline.

They released me because there weren't enough beds.

For nine days I was crucified on an UNHCR foam mattress.

Mother dressed my arm and foot with Rivanol.

At the same time, my father lay in the next room, wounded.

He'd stepped on a landmine which blew off half his foot.

I couldn't wait to have my stitches removed so I could go out.

I was falling apart with boredom.

I started writing poetry:

"Through iron sights I gaze at the stars
As they casually waste their lustre
When they die they don't agonise over their expulsion
From the world and their own flesh
My gun is cock-a-block with sentiment."

Women's War

Nađa is a kid. Greta is an elderly woman. Nađa goes to secondary school, she's not quite a kid but that's how I refer to her. From time to time, her friends visit our refugee home. One of them has a fair complexion, blue eyes. I sometimes think she eyes me furtively, but I pretend not to notice because I am a soldier, a grown man, although I am only about twenty. Then again, it's not proper for kids to fall in love with young adults. I've no time for love; I've devoted myself to other things. Amongst them war, but I've mentioned that more times than one. Comradeship with other soldiers, friends, acquaintances, rakia and weed, but I've mentioned that, too. One might say it's a case of fraternal love between young men, but that's quite beside the point now.

I soon forget about Nađa's friend, for one must press on, one must be mature as long as there's a war on; I've no time for by-the-ways like love. Love, at the moment, is a bit stand-offish towards abstractions such as homeland or nation. There is, however, such thing as true love for things quite concrete and tangible, like home, street or town. Here I mean the lost home, the lost street, the lost town. The town has lost us and we are alone in the universe. It's not the town's fault, and it isn't ours, either.

I don't know what Nađa is thinking about and I don't take her seriously. Nađa spends time with Greta. The two of them live in a world of their own. Greta raised Nađa, she is like a second mother to her. Greta is an elderly woman, very wise and knowledgeable. Nađa and Greta play patience and listen to Radio Rijeka on a set connected to a car battery. Greta is a passionate smoker, she loves crosswords but there aren't any in wartime. Inside the radiobox Andrea Bocelli and Sarah Brightman sing *Time to Say Goodbye*.

It's as though Greta and Nađa were two dispossessed noble-women. Greta, of course, is a countess, Nađa her right hand. They have now been expelled from their county. Nobody knows them; the faces in the street are strange. None treat them with due respect. In turn, the two of them don't much care what people in their new town think about them. Greta and Nađa listen to the news, remembering the number of shells that have fallen on such and such town on a given day. They remember the number of dead and wounded, because we all do. It's an informal sport of sorts, it may become an Olympic discipline someday, and it consists of a radio speaker informing us in a distraught voice that such and such number of howitzer, mortar and cannon shells were fired on town XY during an enemy attack on the very heart of the town. Greta and Nađa are able to tell howitzer and cannon shells from one another, because the former fly a lot longer than the latter and you have time to find cover. They learnt this from our father. At times, radio reports make mention of surface-to-air missiles, which are used – ironically enough – not to shoot down aeroplanes but to destroy our cities and towns. For nothing is the way it may at first seem in war. The missiles have poetic names: Dvina, Neva, Volna. The surface-to-surface missile Luna has the prettiest name. One landed near our house, the blast lifted a few tiles off the roof. Dry snow seeped through the hole in the roof onto the concrete steps carpeted with varicoloured rag-rug. The cold falls into our home vertically.

Greta & Nađa remember all that. Nađa goes to school. Greta stays at home with our mother. Father and I are on the frontline all the time. The radio-sport of remembering the body count and the destruction of towns and cities spreads to every house without exception, be it inhabited by locals, or by refugees. It goes without saying that we, being refugees, couldn't have possibly brought our own houses along on our backs like snails can and do, so the houses we've moved into have become the way we are – homeless, filled with few possessions and many human desires.

Suada, our mother, is the barycentre around which all things and living beings in our home orbit. Apart from Greta & Nada, there is also a little tomcat, as well as a dog that has survived distemper and twitches a bit as he walks. His name is Humpy Horsey, after a character from a Russian fairy tale. Father and I are optional subjects in our refugee family portraits, as we are seldom home.

Suada looks after our civilian lives. Every year she takes a horse cart to a remote village where she plants spuds. The yields range from 500 kg to 700 kg. This guarantees that we won't starve, in case we also don't die in some other way, and the ways to die are many, and they form part of life.

Once I was *detailed* to spade up a patch of the green behind our house. I was at it until Mother saw me toiling and moiling, my face flushed, pushing the blade into the hard soil with the sole of my boot. She snatched the spade from my hands and did the job herself. I was *dismissed*, and I could go out, where my mates were, were the alcohol was.

Suada procured not only victuals but also articles of clothing to meet our modest needs. Thus I was *issued* a terry robe with an aitch emblazoned on the chest, and I called it Helmut. A kind-hearted Helmut donated his robe and helped me feel a bit like a human being. It's not advisable to feel like too much of a human being though, lest your being assume an air of haughtiness, and you become toffee-nosed, as they say in the vernacular. A being could get all kinds of ideas into its head. It might lust after this or that, and there is neither this nor that to be got in the new town. Unless you have a lot of money. Still, even with money, many pleasures remain out of reach, and all they do is feed our fancy and lend us faith in a future better than counting shells and remembering body counts.

That is the main sport in our County. It's just about to go Olympic.

Nađa grows and goes to school. Greta is always the same. Patience, news and Radio Rijeka playlists shape their time. They have a room of their own – they may have been expelled from their lands, but they've retained some trappings of nobility. Greta sends Nađa out to survey the prices of foodstuffs on the black market, things such as oranges, juice, chocolate. Nađa returns and briefs Greta, who decides what will be purchased. Sometimes Nađa fetches ingredients and Greta bakes a cake. This happens when Greta receives money from her relatives in Slovenia. The two of them have a special nook in the wardrobe where they stash their goodies. Inside the radio, the blind Andrea Bocelli and Sarah Brightman sing *Time to Say Goodbye*.

Suada looks after the house and all the living beings in and around it. The little tom is becoming less and less little. At some point I can no longer remember what happens to him, he vanishes into a mysterious feline land, far from the radio reports, far from the laundry soap with which we wash our hair, far from the bath tub mounted on four bricks, far from the cold tiles of the toilet in which I often see my face, distorted with weed and alcohol because it cannot be otherwise. It is the same bathtub in which Mum washed the shot-through blood-encrusted camo vest I strutted about in during nocturnal piss-ups, flaunting my spoils. I'd stripped a dead Autonomist, as if I was about to wash him and wrap him in a white shroud for funeral. But he remained lying on the melting crust of snow on a slope overgrown with stunted conifers. Almost naked, in his pants and boots with socks showing. He lay there for a few days before somebody thought we should bury him, then dig him up again to swap him for victuals. For we were made by nature, and to nature we shall return, naked like the day we were born.

Nađa goes to school, and school, like war, drags on forever. Greta plays patience, feeds Humpy Horsie, feeds the tom who pops down from the mysterious feline land every now and then because he misses us (at least I like to think so), and the birds, for Greta loves all living beings.

Suada picks pigweed in the dales and meadows. She is a pigweed gatherer, in pigweed dwelleth iron, and iron we need to keep the blood red. Greta and Nađa may well be blue-blooded, what with that room of their own, whilst Mum, Dad and I sleep in the sitting room. The tom slept there, too, before he broke away to live a life of roaming and roving. When he was little he would stalk me, and when I blinked in my sleep he'd give me a brush with his paw. Humpy Horsie is growing up and twitches less and less. Prognoses are good for Humpy, even the end of war may be in sight, but we cannot afford to have such high hopes, we are not accustomed to such luxury. Therefore we cannot allow ourselves to entertain fancies and reveries about a better world that is to come. We are wholly accustomed to this one, like a lunatic is used to his strait-jacket. Although all fighters are wont to declare that they would get killed in action eventually, deep inside I believe I will survive, but I don't say it because I don't want to jinx myself.

Smirna is a pal of mine. She works as a waitress, rumour has it she moonlights as a prostitute, which is of no consequence to me as I'm not interested in rumours, even if they're true. I'm interested in human beings as such, and Smirna is one, and so am I. Majority opinions don't interest me, I don't cave under peer pressure, I rely on what my heart tells me. The only difference between the two of us is that she isn't a refugee. Smirna likes to read, I've lent her a copy of Mishima's novel *The Sailor Who Fell from Grace with the Sea*. She'll likely never return it, there's a war on, who would remember to return a borrowed book in times like these? I remember the closing sentence: *Glory, as anyone knows, is bitter stuff.*

Zuhra, known as Zu, is a friend of mine. We've known each other *since before the war*. When you say since before the war, it's as though you remembered that you once used to live in a lost kingdom, the same one in which Greta & Nađa had been noblewomen. In the days of the Kingdom of Before-the-War, Zuhra worked at a video rental, I rented tapes at her shop. We listened to the same music, we patronised the same regal café. She once sent me a beer with a dedication note to the frontline. Zuhra is young and combative, she doesn't lack optimism. We listen to grunge music, we drink beer and rakia. It makes us happy. Although we are young, we know full well that there's something missing. Someone has taken something from us and refuses to give it back. We don't know what that something is called, or what it looks like, but we do know it's something very important for our young lives. Older adults feel the same way, they, too, have had something taken away from them, they, too, don't know what it's called or what it looks like. When someone takes something like that away from you, it's too late for common sense. The only thing you know is that there's a hole that's getting larger and larger and there's nothing you can fill it with.

Zuhra is strong enough not to think about these things. That's what we're both like, that's why we're friends. We've known each other since the days of the Kingdom of Before-the-War. We like to spend time together because it makes us feel that the hole in and around us is shrinking, if only by a smidgen.

Azra, too, is strong and upright. She is tall and beautiful in a special way. I was on a perilous line once, beech and hornbeam trees outside were crackling with cold, Azra phoned me via the brigade phone exchange. One flick of the switch on the switchboard, and we were transported to a realm of magic where nothing was impossible. She was at home, her civilian receiver in hand. I was in a dugout, holding the olive-green receiver of a military field phone. I keep it away from my ear; the phone is prone to tiny electrical surges that zap the ear-lobe. During my stint at that line on Padež Hill I wore Azra's turquoise scarf. It held the smell of her skin and the swoosh of unknown seas, a memory of all the kingdoms we lost, and all the ones we might someday regain.

I envy her for the fact that her family home is intact. All things inside are in the same place all the time: the photographs on the wall, the telly, the sofa, the armchairs, the tables, the doors, the shelves above the basin in the bathroom. Immobility is a virtue. When you get uprooted from your pot and forcefully transplanted into another one, all you want to do is strike root and stay put. Books gather dust as if the war never happened. Azra's house keeps the memory of a bygone peace. It *is* peace. When I come over and talk to her parents I feel like a phantom. As if I'm making things up when I say that we, too, had a house and a flat before the war, a family history of our own, that is now undocumented, since we no longer have any photos.

Azra works at a café, I'm constantly on the frontline. Sometimes, on leave, I drink at her work and I don't pay. With her wages she's bought a pair of Adibax trainers, and we admire them, although the brand name betrays a counterfeit. Matters not, the trainers are new, fashionably designed, worthy of admiration. Sometimes she buys a Milka chocolate and a can of proper coke for each of us, and we give our mates the slip. We hide behind the wooden huts where smuggled consumer goods are sold, and we greedily eat the chocolate and drink the coke. That is also how we make love, furtively, in places secret and dark. Azra keeps me alive by loving me.

I have a higher purpose now, something loftier than bare life and the struggle for survival.

Dina is a strong, brave young woman. She has a child with the same name as me. I used to see her around in the Kingdom of Before-the-War. I was younger than her and we were never formally introduced, the great generational gaps that existed in that realm were difficult to close. Black-and-white was the kingdom, it was the eighties, films with happy endings, New Wave.

Dina works in catering, like Azra and Smirna, due to the circumstances. We're sitting in the garden of her refugee house. We're drinking instant powder juice from jars: glasses are superfluous in war. All glasses are broken, all hands bloody. As Azra and I kiss feverishly, our bodies intertwined like in the sculpture *Laocoön and His Sons*, Dina's son darts towards the road wanting to hug a car, but Dina catches him in the nick of time and my little namesake is safe. Azra and I were charged with keeping an eye on him, but our kisses took us far from reality. We drink Step Light instant juice from pickles jars, because we've been expelled from our empires, and now we can be barbarians if we jolly well please. We're entitled to all kinds of behaviour, and getting a-rude and a-reckless is just our style. We all fight in our own way. Women's war is invisible and silent, but it is of vast importance, though we men on the frontline selfishly think we matter the most. There are women medics and women fighters on the frontlines. I can never forget a young female fighter I once saw, and her firm, confident gait. From one of her shins, through a tear in her uniform trousers, jutted out the nickel-plated bars of a fixation device.

Greta & Nađa play patience. Suada manages the planets of our household solar system. Azra, Dina and Smirna work at their cafés. Zuhra waits for her brother to return from the front. She also waits for us, her friends, to return so we can hang about. Somehow, all things grow and eventually collapse, like a great big wave when it finally reaches the shore. Someone in us plays patience, goes to school, does chores, washes up in a smoky boozer, goes to the front, digs spuds, someone in us laughs at us and our lives. We have an ancient life force inside, and it refuses to leave us. The blind Andrea Bocelli and Sara Brightman sing *Time to Say Goodbye*.

There is this Story

There is this line stretching through the wood like the intestines of a boar when you open it with a burst and steam rises from the puddle of undigested feed.

There are dugouts with stovepipes in lieu of chimneys which we brought from the burnt-out houses.

There is the two-day corpse whose innards have been eaten by feral pigs. He used to herd them.

There is the dead enemy soldier by the school, whoever walks past blasts his head with bullets.

There are guns and bombs and bullets in black magazines.

There are trees which we burn in tin stovelets sending them straight to the arboreal heaven. On their way they pass through clouds devoid of any purpose except to glide unflaggingly like the flat line on an EKG screen.

There was, for a while, patriotism in me, then everything went to shite.

There is the dogged resolution to defend this line and this wood because they exist precisely for us to be here and defend them.

There are coats of arms, standards, ranks, financial bonuses, military formations, wartime rapture, patriotic songs, armpit sweat and the entire machinery designed to lift up morale like an old man's prick.

There are the three seconds it takes for a Yugoslav hand grenade to go off.

There are the implements of death, and we are here to make use of them, otherwise everything would be pointless, like the beck between those two hillocks; it is there as a random or divinely willed decoration, no difference to me.

There are the small chub in the stream's meanders, feeding on flies, squeezing into the roots of the willows, dredging the bottom for crawfish, they spend their lives there lending the stream a flowing sense of sense. Fragrant mint grows on the banks.

There is the tree with the unexploded percussion-fuse rifle grenade stuck into it like when you say: Enes Shock died from shrapnel.

There is this constellation of leaves – if I may be permitted a metaphor – through which I poke my sweaty head in fear of the all-seeing sniper.

There is the dog licking the haemorrhoid blood off the turd I shat out behind the shed this morning.

There is the book titled *An Anthology of Contemporary American Poetry* which I stole from the library.

There is me in camo uniform sitting on the forest floor hunching over American poetry like our Partisan poet Vladimir Nazor during the calm between two battles.

There is Allen Ginsberg and the excerpts from his poem *Howl* which I learnt by heart.

There were so many days on leave when I was so drunk I don't understand how I didn't die from cirrhosis.

There are a host of poets who have written about death; I have nothing to add, I don't know death personally.

There is the snow camo over we found in the attic of an "Autonomist" house during a routine search. Crusted blood flaked off the sheer fabric like pointless dust.

There is this dugout with which I've become one, as if it were my native home and hearth.

There is the password, parole, package, pistol, pressure.

There is the night when I mechanically repeat the password staring at the fire because I don't know what else to do.

There is the dawn when I wank off watching the birth of the sun.

There is the Autonomist line, lightly entrenched, which we may attack tomorrow, if the order is given.

There will be the prisoners, the wounded, the dead. I hope I'll survive. Just before the off something will start to flutter in my chest and the weakness will drop down into my stomach like a sip of strong rakia. I don't believe I'll be as brave as Borges's hero Juan Facundo Quiroga. After all, he is just a historical figure from a poem.

There is the girl I love, some thirty kilometres from here, and every time I think of her I'm overcome by pre-mortal fear of never seeing her again.

There is the 60 mm mortar in our unit, called Little Hasib, and a dozen shells we keep like jewels from the royal crown.

There are the bits of a porker we cook on the rusty grill, high as kites.

There is the giant Kagemusha Shadow Warrior I imagine strutting down the macadam road towards us as we eat the tasty meat.

There are a billion details that escape me now because I'm thinking of Azra's strong, tremulous embrace that can gird an aeon's worth of love and the despair of women waiting for fighters to return from war.

There are the Luna ground-to-ground missiles moaning overhead on their way to Cazin. If I aestheticise the horror, the rockets resemble great balls of fire, but that benefits no one.

There is this story devoid of events.

There was Fikret "Fikro" Avdagić.

There was Mirsad "Ćipo" Mustedenagić.

There was Samir "Bale" Redžić.

There was Osman Jakupović.

There was Enes "Shock" Hadžifejzagić.

There was Hari Palić.

There was Emili.

There was Merfin Pađen.

There was Refko Ramić.

There was Zlatko Bajšanski.

There was Sakib Novkinić.

There was Himzo Alijagić.

There was Speci.

There was Smajo Hasanović.

There was Vejsil "Deba" Šarić.

There was Zijad "Zica" Hasanović, brother of Smajo Hasanović.

There was Hamdija "Whitey" Spahić.

There was Hafura.

There was Redžo Begić.

There was Seduan Šarić.

There was Selmir "Julio" Šarić.

There was Ibraga "Dasa" Hadžić.

There was Irfan Kadić.

There was Mirsad Crnkić.

There was Kusur.

There was Zijo Kabiljagić.

There was Ismet "Ipo" Arnautović, the brother of Zuhra.

There was Šefko Begić.

There was Amir "Amko" Sivić.

There was Enis Duranović, known as Eno the Whippet.

There was Vlado Remić.

There was Đenad "Đeno" Redžić.

There was Sado Redžić.

There was Arif Suljić.

There was Hasan "Globehead" Burmić.

There was Mirsad Ekić.

There was Samir "Baja" Sefić.

There was Sead "The Godfather" Harambašić.

There was Huska Spahić,

There was Refik "Ruma" Suljić...

There are the soldiers' cemeteries Ometaljka, Soline, and many others all over the County of Bihać.

There is this story in which nothing happens, for *what great progress we've made during this particular war in the art of invisibility.*

DARK UND DARK

The Great Dream

I blew my last fifty marks and became a prole. I had had thirteen glasses of Žilavka wine, three dark lagers and five draughts of Laško beer. At seven twenty-two in the morning I was awoken by a medium-heavy hangover. I knew the cure, I reached under the table and took *The Communist Manifesto*, translated by Moša Pijade during his days in the Lepoglava prison, with the foreword by Slavoj Žižek titled *The Spectre is Still Haunting*. I read the last third of the book and fell asleep overcome by revolutionary zeal.

I didn't dream of anything. Or rather, I couldn't remember dreaming of anything. Back then I scorched my memory centre too often at night, only to discover a chasm in my brain the next morning. I was nagged by persistent heartburn. I drank water from a blue plastic cup, that came free with the 1 kg packet of Cedevita instant orange juice powder. The glass stood sentry like a lone house of God on the mirror-slick table to my right as I rotted away, carefully cultivating my hangover, in the squeaky bed in my ground floor flat in Soukbunar, overlooking Sarajevo. To my left was a painted wall.

I got up and found a squishy lemon in my Obodin fridge. I quaffed the lemonade down, slurped up the sugar and the chopped up pips from the bottom of the cup. I put on a terry-cloth house robe. Turned on my laptop, popped *Every Woman Has a Fantasy 3* into the CD-ROM drive and had a wank, thus killing the libido in me that had been boosted by ethanol metabolised in my system. With my slipper I rubbed the sperm into the faux carpet. On the fridge

I ate the leftovers of cheese pie and a piece of a pickled green chilli pepper with stem. I wolfed down a wedge of Zdenka melted cheese like a dog swallowing a fly. I crumpled up the plastic bag and paper wrap the pie came in. Chucked the ball in the bin. Swilled it all down with cold water. If I'd had some yoghurt to warm the heart, or some sauerkraut, I would've ended up with a groggy robot body yet again. For the calisthenics exercises I remembered from my time in the Yugoslav Army – press ups, lizard lunges, squats – I had no strength in me. Fuck a healthy body in a healthy mind – that's a Nazi slogan. I tried to read Różewicz, it wasn't a smooth read, he seemed too pathetic. His words were unconvincing, or perhaps my brain was too numb and unfeeling. The brain, after all, is the supreme organ. *This train will not leave my memory. All the living are guilty. Guilty are little children who offered bouquets of flowers. The dead will not rehabilitate us.* These verses glided down my crucified yet unredeeming nerve cells, but you could still base a religion around them. Ganglia dying for our sins. Especially those that have to do with booze, drugs and fornication. Peace, love, serenity. The Ssssuuubliiimeee Ganglion loves you (the voice has got to be nasal)! Its body and spirit, its erythrocytes transformed into the sulphur wine from the isle of Vis. By the blessed heart of Baby Ganglion! Great is the wrath of Lord Neurite!

I replaced the book under the massive table. The electric fire, which I had to hotwire to turn it on as it sparked pink, was poking out from under the portable black-and-white TV I swapped for a pair of light-up trainers. The trainers exceeded the value of the telly, pegged at ten marks, and the remainder was paid to me in *burek* credits at the pie shop "Aperitiv". The TV was centred at the edge of the table to be parallel with my knees when I'm in bed. The room reeked of synthetic socks; I hadn't taken my bright red Adidas trainers off all day.

I decided to take a bath and wash off the alcohol film as well as the feeling of guilt based on nothing in particular yet omnipresent like the dust, hair and my dead skin cells on the floor and the neatly arranged books. In this biosphere, bacteria and mites reigned supreme.

Maybe that would liven up my muscles a bit, maybe it would get my blood happily coursing through my arteries. At any rate, I would ameliorate the after-effects of drunkenness with Nivea shampoo and an aromatherapy soap which revitalises and relaxes. *Calm your senses & soften your skin.* As I sit in the slimy, thirty-year-old tub, I'd be staring at the belly of the boiler, with a jet of hot water, I'd be massaging my head, my back, my torso, and my penis and testicles. I would greedily gasp for air saturated with humidity, breathe it in like precious puffs of weed. I would listen to my heart beat. The hydro massage would last for as long as there is water in the steel belly of the Tiki boiler. I would endeavour not to think anything, what the fuck is the use of a thought scorched with hot aqua? These are moments to get rid of the stress caused by the volcanic acceleration of life.

Acceleration times mass equals force, so I learnt in the science class. I would rub my arms, legs, hair, genitals and other surfaces with a torn up towel with the old coat of arms – six fleurs-de-lys on an escutcheon – in relief. Two fleurs-de-lys had holes in them; I could stick my fingers through.

I dried my feet, stepped out of the tub and into the tartan slippers punctured by the power of the toes. I put on a pair of boxers, opened the fly button to let the steam evaporate. I rubbed my armpits and underchin with the bell end of the roll-on deodorant. With my fingers I styled my hair like a Russian *muzhik* from the film *Andrei Rublev*. (Just so it's clear that I can make cinematic references.) Later I would brush my teeth with Zirodent toothpaste filled with active capsules of burgundy and green. These capsules have certain powers as regards the gums and the teeth. I didn't read the instructions very thoroughly, but at any rate, things are exactly the opposite of what the Quality Control Institute claims. I was so incisive, it was morning, and in the morning we are friends of the muses – *musis amici* in Latin. Though I could also be the devil's protégé, seeing that I'd been enjoying drink & other vices the night before.

To rake the eyebrows with a plastic comb. To rinse coily hairs down the tub. To save the spider holding on for life in front of the cross-shaped drain hole. To put on the threadbare hybrid between pyjama and tracksuit bottoms. To cloak self in terrycloth robe like an indoor samurai of Soukbunar. To go for a walk around the flat with my hands on my back. To be Rodinesquelly pensive. To play with dovetailed fingers. To measure in paces the room which is the kitchen, the sitting room and the bedroom. To laser-scan the titles of the books lined up on the shelves of the old-fashioned cabinet. Above the books are coffee cups emblazoned with "Grandpa" in brown letters, and a set of china. To sit at the kitchen table where the laptop is emplaced. To revise the most recent writing. To seek out synonyms of adjectives, verbs and nouns. To think about punctuation. About sentence rhythm and the frequency of conjunctions. To increase font size and read, for the umpteenth time, the 978-word story titled *March of the Dead*. To be surgically precise, merciless to the extraneous text. To reach the conclusion that I've finished a short story collection, because writing about war has temporarily drained me.

To think of the structure of the book which resembles the EKG tracings of a healthy heart. The peaks and valleys are stories of different emotional timbre, pace and rhythm. To feel the draw of the long prose form with plenty of poetry thrown in. To shut down the computer by pressing the silver button.

To get dressed and descend into the city, towards new triumphs of labour. To borrow money or run a tab. To eat nothing at all, unless there is mezze of olives and cheese. Start with coffee, finish with beer and tequila. Smoke six or seven joints, not spliffs, rolled into a skin the colour of dried tobacco leaf. To talk to some foreign woman at the bar in drunken English. To rock on your feet in an underground café, aware that the universe is cracking. To sweat three hundred and fifty thousand sweats at once. To come up for air running away from the walls closing in. To vomit all night on the terrace of the jazz club *Clou*, sitting shirtless on the concrete wall, listening to the mellifluous patter of raindrops on the sheer green asbestos of the awning.

I wanted to squeeze out that booze turd but I couldn't stand up straight. I was scanning around for some nook to rid myself of the gastro-intestinal discomfort. The weed and booze were coming out of all holes. I decided to take a dump in the stairwell. I dragged myself there somehow, but it was too well-lit, too much traffic. I darted down furiously to the mouldy toilet, bouncing off the walls like a steel pinball in the machine. I vacated my bowels. No toilet paper, no water. I wished I had some leaves. I found a packet of paper handkerchiefs behind the bowl and wiped my arse. I came up again. The air had become refreshing. The rain is doing what it's supposed to do. I dunked my face into my palms on my knees. Tried to fall asleep. Just before morning I stepped out into the rain-washed street with the barman, and sat on the sill of the *KTK Shoes* window. Scroungers were poncing by the hatch of the open-all-hours shop. My mind cleared up suddenly. I went straight down the street opposite. I don't remember the walk home. I undressed down to my boxers and pulled up a heavy eiderdown.

Let the ruling classes tremble at a communist revolution. The proletarians have nothing to lose but their chains. They have a world to win. The sentences thundered from the viscous horizon of mercury clouds. Moša Pijade shouted through a flaring bullhorn: Workers of the world unite!

In the dark shone a heart-shaped bum like the silver belly of a rainbow trout. I heard a myriad of voices, shrapnel letters bouncing off the incandescent skull of the planet. Somebody was smashing the typewriter. Somebody fluid and immense like a God of Alcohol.

A Cockwork Orange

Fucked off by women and tossed into life, I was suffering from a severe form of shagzophrenia. I diagnosed myself and thought of a name for my disorder. Booze came as a by-product of a physical, emotional and moral split.

I was overcome by an insane sense of solitude. I'd always been surrounded by crowds of people. It is precisely in those moments that a feeling billows up in you, all the horror of a beatnik existence. You talk and you drink, the table is laden with glasses and bottles, an ashtray the size of a baking dish is filled with suffocated fags. Nothingness glistens in our eyes, those computerised gazes in which you can see the moment just before the Big Bang boomed and the cosmic skein started to unravel. We scream with laughter, we're not doing half bad at all, you only live once and other such platitudes allow us to guzzle till kingdom come. Those were the days of competitiveness, an Olympics of joy and anarchistic rapture, suicide, robbery, manslaughter, car accidents. The crime section sucked people's lives in, taking on the role of the monotheist god.

I barged into *Clou*. I was the first punter. Outside it was below the tenth notch below zero. All day I'd been drinking *loza* – grape rakia. I couldn't wait for the jazz pit to open.

Above the wooden bar glowed a neon guitar and a neon *Bud Beer* logo covered with a piece of bamboo screen. Dim bulbs in different colours stuck to the walls like bats in a cave. Leaning on a wall-mounted table I tilted a bottle of *Laško*. The glue from the label was sticking to my fingers. Every time I heard the thud of the heavy door I turned around expecting to see my messianic girlfriend. I desperately wanted to fall in love. I was stacking a third beer on top of the previous two in my hungry stomach sack. I would've been happy to see anyone at all. I would've hugged the first punter who came in through the door if that meant the evening wouldn't turn out hopelessly tedious and unpromising.

I chatted with the barman, that's how we shattered the silence in the sfumato twilight. Sting or Clapton were playing from invisible loudspeakers. Here things start to happen only after midnight, when hordes of creatures start rushing in on booze, weed or who knows what, in pursuit of post-midnight bliss. I was one of them myself. We are creatures of midnight, celestial *udarniks* steeped in alcohol molecules, in a cyclopic osmosis with the dank, the cold and the dark. Masters of the arts of darkness from noir films. Like Herbert's heavenly proletarians, we carry our wings underarm like violins. Nothing could stop us from playing to the fullest the role of wonderful losers.

Two girls were the embryo of the commotion and the ensuing events. With her long raven hair and big tits in a crocheted sweater, next to me stood a decent and not overly pretty girl. Her looks didn't matter in the end, the drink was doing its thing. The longer I looked at her, the smaller her head became, until it finally shrunk to the size of a coconut. Due to my soaring blood alcohol content, I guess. As I talked to her, I'd nonchalantly graze her milky balloons with my elbow. She didn't flinch back. The skin on her neck was fair and fragrant. Her eyes large, almond-coloured. Her friend found moorings in the haven of a table elsewhere in the room. Our physiological closeness peaked in a bout of furious snogging; it was as though we were discovering a cure for death in each other's lips. I ran my fingers across her trousers, across her bulging fanny, she grabbed my cock, which could've been the mast to hoist a sail to and glide away into the end of the night. I wanted us to go to some stairwell and fuck on our feet. It didn't go beyond the snogging. She was a bit jealous because I was eyeing other female creatures, too.

'You won't be returning to me now, will you?' she'd ask on her way to the ladies'.

My morale dropped, I realised I wouldn't be getting conkers deep. I squired her home, we hopped into a doorway, where the usual odour of ammonia scratched the throat. She sucked me off on the frosty steps. I fixed my gaze to the stalactites of icy tears on the frozen ceiling.

'Nice, that,' I said.

I looked down; she'd stopped gobbling it and was tickling my bollocks. My pubes reeked of billy-goat hair. My cock was semi-tumescent and felt wooden. I wouldn't have felt a thing if she'd bitten it off. Shivers attack me from behind when I remember the scene from Sam Peckinpah's *Cross of Iron* in which the Russian female POW sucks a German soldier's willie, only to bite it off in the end. James Coburn leaves his comrade in arms to bleed in the stable and be lynched by the blue-eyed, big-titted Russians.

I walked her to a tower block with a façade the colour of dirty snow. The wind swept up downy fluffs from the ice-glazed street, threw them onto the sides of our faces. We made an appointment for the next day. The cold was a Singer sewing machine that was stitching through my bollocks and my thigh bones, sticking them with a giant titanium needle.

* * *

She finally popped round, after one failed appointment. I was as pure and sober as Jesus Christ. Her fanny was hot and juicy. I pushed two digits in. She grabbed me by the cock. I wanted her to sit on it. The light bothered her. I carried out the order and turned it off. Everything went fine until she told me I was too impatient, and asked if I had protection? That's when I lost patience. I couldn't get it up again, I was too nervous.

We should've had a few beers before sex. We lay naked on the sofa like Greek statues in the depot of some museum. We were hundreds of light years away from each other. We lit up. She read my just written poems on the black-and-white screen of my old 386 laptop. She cursed our lot and the country we lived in, because I wrote such good poetry, yet I lived in abject poverty. Absolutely romantic!

On her way out she left ten marks on the table. We hadn't even shagged, and there she was giving me money. I was such a sad, bad gigolo. I wasn't any kind of gigolo, I just liked the word. I stared at the ink-stained note. In the corner of the ceiling, a spider was crocheting his murderous lace. Water dripped from the ample trunk of the tap onto the stainless steel bottom of the sink. That liquid metronome clicked a hypnotic beat. The drops huddled together into plump pools. In the smoke rings I was puffing up into the air, I sensed solitude.

The Body is the Dragon's Lair

The body is the temple of the Lord.
John Cazale as Sal Naturale in *Dog Day Afternoon*

We set out for Vrelo Bosne, the picnic site by the headwaters of the river Bosna. The roots of the Bosnian state. Vesna, Amel, and I. We took a tram to Ilidža by the former Maršal Tito barracks. An abysmally hot October southerly was blowing. The news said the wind came from the Sahara, carrying red and yellow grains of desert sand. It had an irritating effect and it instilled anxiety into the bodies of chronic patients.

The tram pushed air, which in turned pushed aquarelle leaves out of the way. High up in the crowns of the plane trees, jackdaws were pitch black against the sky as they balanced nimbly on the thin branches. Their cawing died down under the wheels of the tram. My heart was beating underneath my t-shirt like a sprint racer's, as if I'd been running from a pair of tank tracks that devoured time and space, leaving behind fathomless colourless furrows of devoured life.

I was bothered by the crush in the car. The cloying scent of sweaty bodies gave me chest spasms. Salty droplets dripped down from my hands. I was trying to hide how nervous I was. I was standing next to Amel, and we both held onto the greasy metal bar by the exit. Amel unintentionally grazed with his rucksack the shoulder of a man sitting on a red chair below us. The guy glared at him insanely and told Amel to stop shoving him. Amel was as peaceful as the Buddha and Mahatma Gandhi put together. But I could smell trouble in the air. I told the miffy fellow that we weren't alone, the car was crammed. He looked at me with his dot-like irises.

'Piss the fuck off, cunt!' he said loudly.

Something squeezed my chest. Wave after wave of heat climbed up to my head.

'Are you off your nut, man?'

'Piss the fuck off, cunt!' he repeated.

The inside of the car stretched and contracted as if I'd taken LSD, and I dove headfirst into a kaleidoscope of human flesh, rubber and metal. I punched him as hard as I could on the right eyebrow bone. He fell off his seat. People scattered along the length of the tram as if someone had chucked in a can of tear gas. He got up. A bump the size of a walnut appeared above his right eye. I lamped him again; two or three times in the gob. He stuttered and fell on his back. He was indestructible like Terminator made of liquid metal. He got up again. We started to grapple due to the lack of elbow room. I realised he was stronger than me, but fortunately he didn't know how to fight.

I kneed him in the bollocks. A woman, quite beside herself, was shouting that we should stop, because she had small children. I made the words out through the delirium and the drumming of blood in my temples. I couldn't see anyone except the maniac. The tram stopped at every stop along the way as if nothing had been going on, and people got off. It was soon empty. I forgot about my friends. I was a gladiator in an arena, in mortal combat. He grabbed hold of my neck from behind and repeatedly hit me in the nape with his other fist. I returned blows with my elbow.

'My strength failed me!' I was addressing this epic sentence to myself, in the heat of the moment.

The duke-out ground to a stalemate. The driver stopped the tram at a stop. For a split second, I saw the wrought iron fence opposite, framed by the window, and beyond it the leafy spindles – poplars in the wind. The lunatic was trying to push me out of the tram. I grabbed the bar. Inertia threw him and he tumbled out. We cursed a blue streak at each other. I dared him to step back in, he dared me to step out. Neither dared cross the magical demarcation line.

'Go home, gobshite! Let your wife see the absolute state of you!'

The veins on his neck popped out like the crests of the reptiles from the Galapagos Islands. His face was contorted and swollen. He almost sprouted a pair of antlers. If we'd been fighting in the ring I would've won by technical KO, although we weren't nearly the same category. He had twenty kilos on me, he was close to forty, in his prime. His handgrip was so long he could clasp his fingers around my neck.

My head was throbbing from all the blows I took. I had red bruises and sores on my throat and below my ears, where he'd been strangling me at some point. If I'd had a knife I would've gutted him like a fish, turned him into fillets.

The tram moved on. I glanced through the cloudy window, we were passing by the city transport company. The bout had lasted seven or eight stops. Although it felt like three seconds to me. At Ilidža I met Amel and Vesna. Vesna said her knees hadn't been shaking like that since the war.

Abandon any hope of ever escaping the war, ye who have survived it.

I popped three five-milligram diazepams. My muscles relaxed. The tremor was gone. When I got back home in the suburb of Tranzit, I immediately made 30 press-ups in one sitting. I could feel encrusted blood in my hair with my fingertips. I was a hero in an out-of-tune era. The sedatives had a superficial effect.

I breathed deeply to steady my heart beat. I looked at the furrows of bruises in the mirror. I feed the fish in the aquarium. I checked the water temperature. I baby-talked the two cleaners,

Boško Buha and Mika Bosnić (named after WW2 heroes), who were kipping motionless on the smooth pebbles at the bottom. From the anus of Big Bertha the Goldfish trailed a thread of shite, in places crimped by the fish's feeble sphincter. The cleaners were charged with faeces disposal.

I used to love that aquarium and its inhabitants. Fish-spotting. That was my most effective therapy against the constant fear of death which manifested itself in a stabbing sensation in the area around the heart, shortness of breath and high blood pressure. The latter once led me to six days of abstinence, because I thought I'd get a heart attack during intercourse.

I told Nino, my flatmate, about the fight. Paced up and down the place, pleased with the outcome of the fight, feeling my swollen body through which adrenalin coursed furiously. Two years after the war I was still as crazy as Bruce Lee when he licks his own blood off his fingers.

We Sprung from the Loins of the Moon

I fell in love with a woman from a jumbo poster. Her name is *Rilken Silken Color*. One advertising verse was written below her fantastic face: *Hair Color That Excites!*

Teenage girls paraded by the fountain, coquettishly swinging their bums, flashing the flesh of their tiny little bellies and the taut skin of their hips. A piercing on a sun-tanned navel is the pistil of the most fragrant honey flower. Walking orchids, marigolds, daisies, freesias, gardenias and birds of paradise were walking past and being scanned by my eyes. My head was spinning like a fan, trying to take in all the tits & arse around me & all the smug faces with the cute little eyes. I'm a proper dirty filthy thirty-three-year old, shame on me.

It's hard to fight your own body. What spiritual skill has ever overpowered a nocturnal emission? Did the saints and ascetics have control over their cocks? Anything is possible, except a wooden stove, and even a wooden stove could hold one fire, pontificates the folksy witticism. I fantasised about the Rilken Woman, her noble, made-up features, her seductive lenses that burn their way into your brain and scorch its curls and coils, her nose, worthy of princess Esmeralda from the soapy fairy tale. In my eyes, Rilken Woman was the mistress of the universe and the explosive sex cells.

I decided to take a walk staring only at the tarmac below, with a view to finding a one mark coin, or at least a fifty pfennig one. One should do something useful, not just gawp at ample-arsed individuals. Autosuggestion is a magical technique, except it can't sate hunger or enlarge the figures in your current account. This is precisely why people read self-help literature. They are essentially a shower of masochists, bollockless tortoises on two legs seeking salvation on this flaming planet where not even platypuses are left alone and just like koalas, sloths, pandas, seahorses, swatch medusas and other care-free creatures, they're being inculcated with the ideology of turbo-folk capitalism. The Dollar, not beauty, changed the world.

Having delivered this inspired prologue, I shall now recount, my magnificent readers, the history of a utopian night:

AT OLIVE'S

We glide down the Vrazova street looking for a last chance. We turn left, to the right of us is the community health centre, we pop into a passage, a shelter for alkies and nutters. It reeks of fresh piss. Dried-out turd piles, like urns full of remains of miserable meals, are dumped by the walls. The wind fraternises them with dust and sweeps them away. Crumpled up leaves of newspaper reveal the shitty reliefs of anuses. Beer bottles lie strewn about like cannon shell casings. We enter an Austro-Hungarian courtyard between two buildings. In front of us is a file of sheet metal garages from the era of *Socialism with a Human Face*: they're lined up neatly like domino tiles. Inside, cars, nails, spanners, grinders, drills, shovels, picks, Wellington boots and bikes rot away, conscientiously gathering dust. Robigus, Różewicz's daemon of rust, is relentless.

These garages belong to the so-called small, family man. It is terrifying to think what these quiet, humble custodians of family values are capable of in times of war. The inside of each garage is a metaphor for the soul of its owner – ultra-pedantry that can turn to insanity worthy of the *Guinness Book of Records* in no time.

One-metre beech logs are lined up against the wall like giant matches. Growth rings can't be seen on the section, because the humidity condenses into mouldy blue-green. We are surrounded by walls with elongated windows that look like loop-holes. Ironclad proof of the military organisation of an architectural cosmos.

Plaster is flaking off near the toilets revealing the progress of the damp. We take a right through a dark tunnel and we reach a front door. The smell is a lot less harsh than in the tunnel – you can tell people live there. Our guide bangs his fist on the rotting wood, just where someone has written in fluorescent marker, "Welcome, thank you, come again!" A voluminous maize cob of a man in blue overalls opens the door. The landlord. His codename is Olive. He weighs round 100 kg, is 170 cm tall, over fifty years of age. His swag belly is the size of a wrecking ball. His untamed toenails jut out from his disintegrating leather sandals, looking like they're made out of clay. His nose a purple pepper. His hair sparse, as grey as his face, crumpled up from incessant drinking. An alcoholic superhero.

We stepped into Olive's. He's turned his flat into a hostelry. To marry business with pleasure. Through an anteroom with squeaky floorboards we reach the main room. We find two rickety sofas furnished with quilts and cushions. You can take a quick kip if you're tired. Between the two sofas is a low table and a few ancient classroom chairs. The carpet has fag burns and chewing gum incrustations. Everyone is looking for the best spot to lean back. A washing line stretches above our heads. There are neckties pegged to it. Among the ties the odd sock, with lycra, the kind that temporarily stop the circulation and make your feet sweat like in a microwave. The walls are embalmed with nicotine as well as human and alcohol fumes. This is what prehistoric caves looked like. Guitars, sparsely strung with gut strings, hang from the walls of Olive's Altamira. Mostly for the show, it seems. And the ties are the quintessential jovial gentleman's accessories. No need for paintings on the walls. Maybe a few Wiehler gobelins, or an aquatint of a crying Gypsy boy, or an idyllical scene of Victorian England would complete the picture. However, in this place everything is a fresco painted by time and accident. The Fat God of Alcohol hovers in the air. If he perches on someone's head, that guy instantly gets a black hole in his memory.

Olive walks up to us. He has draped a dirty, greasy towel across the top of his hand.

'Lads, what'll I get ya?'

'What've you got?'

'We have Zvečevo cognac,' says Olive, as if offering us some divine wine.

That cognac is godly, when you get drunk on it you could kill your own offspring without any remorse, which, according to the scriptures, the Creator himself did quite often.

'Got any bitter, or loza?'

'Just the cognac.'

'How much is the paint thinner?'

'One mark a shot.'

'Give us all a round then.'

Olive goes to the kitchen. He returns with a tray, and on it some shot glasses that look as if someone has just pulled them out of their anus. Light brown with streaks of green. Those must be the alcohol algae, never before beheld by human eye.

Migz picks up a three-string guitar. He mixes blues and Bosnian Sevdah. The glasses are filled and emptied. For a moment we reach the kind of bliss felt by a foetus in amniotic fluid. Olive is drinking too; he's the barkeeper and a guest at the same time. He's robbing Peter to pay Peter.

From the kitchen comes the no transmission pip of a radio station. It's like a distorted guitar humming in your head during a heavy hangover. Water from the bollocksed tap which looks like a giraffe's neck is drumming on a pyramid of dishes. The reed-insulated ceiling in the water closet is caving in and hangs over the toilet bowl like the sword of Damocles. Water trickles down the burry blade, persistent moss grows. If you miss the toilet gates and open the second door to the right, you will find yourself in a bedroom lit by the flashes from a black-and-white TV, as the established light is switched off. A gothic *romancero* set in a hundred year old building from the days of the black and yellow monarchy.

'Olive, give us another round.'

'I'm out of booze,' whimpers Olive.

'Where the fuck do we go now, it's almost dawn?'

'Nah,' says Olive 'we wait for the shop to open and we stock up.'

Olive passes a straw hat around, and we all toss in a mark or two. Piss artists' solidarity is stronger than global capitalism. No one is stingy, no one looks out for himself only. We are in a state of weightlessness, and were we not indoors, we would probably hold hands and take off towards the Milky Way.

Outside, pigeons patiently coo and shit as they wait for the sun underneath the awning. The sky looks like someone has painted it with copper sulphate. The plush curtains which are supposed to protect us from external light become threadbare like the ethereal tissue of ghosts. I would love to teleport myself back to my lair, but I lost my Star Trek badge last night.

Olive goes to the shop, to fetch us more methanol. I wish to thank Borges for his poetry, for I am about to borrow the closing verses of his poem *Temptation* which is about the heroic death of general Juan Facundo Quiroga. *Why end the story that's already been forever told? The carriage sets out for Barranca Yaco.*

So, This is a Novel

With my index finger I flicked an invisible lever on my temple and started the time machine in my head. The leaves of the calendar fall off like tufts of hair after chemo. Memories, my memories, wherefore are ye more significant than the memories of others? It is March, the year 1994, we're sitting by the entrance to Café Ferrari, we're smoking weed, wheezing with laughter. In a circle of twenty metres round our table, the range of the sound waves of our words, people on the terrace stretch their lips, wrinkles around their eyes flare into fans. Directly opposite, some two hundred metres as the crow flies, is the old traditional-style Bosnian house, the birth house of Nurija Pozderac, the WWII volunteer-hero.

'Long live Nurija, the legendary anti-fascist!'

'He's dead,' Žile tells me.

'Well, then, long live Nurija, the legendary Partisan with a star on his cap – posthumously!'

'Fuck him, better look after your health!'

'Death to fascism and the purple people!'

'Freedom is a hydrogen washing machine!'

Zuhra returns from the bar with four beers. We tilt the bottles of hop juice like Popeye the Sailor tilts his spinach tin.

Enter Ćipo.

'Hara Pašin says all squad and platoon commanders and other fighters must gather at the bus station at three o'clock when the bus from Skokovi arrives,' reports Ćipo. 'But fuck the line, I'm not going either, if I see Hara I'll tell him I didn't see you.'

Dead serious, I get up and head home.

'Where are you going?' asks Zuhra, after silence fell and laughter fizzled out in the pleasant air.

'I'm going to Hasin vrh, to leave my bones there.'

I felt some slimy pins and needles on the skin of my face.

1. At home I put on my uniform and my tactical vest, took my Kalashnikov and my tactical rucksack in which I had two locally manufactured hand grenades and a pair of heavy woollen knee-high socks.
2. I washed my hands and my face.
3. All of the above I did with the confidence of an android.
4. I said good-bye to my mum and old man and headed to the bus station.
5. Said good-bye to the four winds.
6. Returned my life to the quartermaster.

I went to the rendezvous point by the petrol station and gazed at the empty ironwork's halls.

I slung my rifle across my shoulder as if at sentry.

Some hundred metres from me, in the neighbourhood of Ćuprija, heavy automatic fire resounded.

Not a soul in the street.

Only the army flag flying on a mast on the factory grounds showed a sign of life.

There were just a few kafanas in that neighbourhood, the turf of the fighters from Sanski Most.

The great big brick chimney was a metaphor of solitude and nothingness.

Further down in the direction of the village of Ćoralići, the metal chimney of the Incel factory was leaning like the Tower of Pisa, because a Yugoslav People's Army J-21 Jastreb nicked it with its wing when it crashed.

The shots weren't subsiding, it sounded like street fighting, every man for himself.

I wasn't moving, the weed pinned me to the spot.

A white Mercedes appeared from the direction of Ćuprija and glided slowly towards me.

When it neared I saw the driver's head resting on the wheel upholstered with perforated leather.

When it drove past me I saw that the driver was covered in blood from the neck down.

He was wearing a white pin-striped waiter's shirt.

The Mercedes slammed head-on into the air machine from which hoses were sticking out.

The machine tipped over and the wheels of the car were spinning in the air.

The man was *asleep* at the wheel.

Žilo came along, on his way to the frontline.

The wheels were humming in the air.

I snapped out of lethargy. We moved the casualty from the driver's to the back seat.

Some bald-headed passer-by asked what to do.

I told him to sit behind the wheel and take the casualty to hospital.

He got into the car and, befuddled by panic, hit the accelerator. The Merc was furiously trying to take off from the air machine into the March sky. The man's glistening skull broke into tiny marbles of sweat.

'Reverse, reverse!' shouted Žilo.

The bloke managed to shift into reverse and get the Mercedes onto the tarmac.

'Are you coming along?'

'No, I have to go to the frontline.'

To leave my bones there – the line went through my head.

The shooting stopped, out of the blue, just like it had started.

It had its own clockwork, an elusive will of its own.

I was standing stiff as a board by the toppled metal rectangle that was oozing engine oil.

I boarded the bus.

The men were dejected, as if going to their own funeral.

You could only hear the revving of the engine and the grinding of the transmission.

'What the fuck is wrong with you, we're not going to our graves, are we?'

I was under full effects of weed, I didn't give a fuck about getting killed.

An oily smegma of dusk was seeping into dugout 2, at the acme.

The next day at nine fifty in the morning a combined arms artillery/infantry attack commenced.[1]

Lying in hospital, after the first shot of opioids, I remembered the enemy soldier who nimbly skipped the stone breastwork and started firing at the blanket hanging on the entrance to the abandoned dugout. He was wearing a five-colour patterned uniform. I threw a green grenade at him, and I never saw him again. Mine was the stronger Pokemon.

I switched the time machine off and lit up.

Ordered an icy Laško beer.

In the park, in front of the café, pigeons were grazing red fruits of afro-shaped bushes. Sinewy branches bent under their weight.

On the first floor balcony a pensioner released a ladybird from a matchbox onto his liver-spotted hand.

One floor above him, a satellite dish was mounted to the railing of the balcony from which the mouldy crust of façade was crumbling away.

---

1   These events are described in the story 'Now We Get a-Rude and a-Reckless'.

The metal Frisbee had "Gazija" written across in green letters.

Two teenagers on the third floor balcony were sparking up a fat zoot.

Coffee, cigarettes, beer, pissing, loza, banal conversations, drunkenness, aching head, crushed body, shit-fuck-cock-piss-cunt…

Trifles of everyday gleamed before my eyes.

THE PHANTOM OF LIBERTY

The Miljacka river flows through our dreams. It carries footballs, plastic 1.5 l coke bottles, a Barbie doll's dishevelled head. In October, leaves soaked in human faeces drift on the surface. It carries adolescent chub and barbell down to the river Bosna, corpses of lonely men and women with bulging piscine eyes, it carries our future from the second hand shop deep into the continent, towards the Black Sea. It flows by Wilson's Promenade, where old people stroll to get away from their first heart attack, where lips are pressed onto lips, where tokes of weed mixed with wine and beer are greedily swallowed. It flows by Wilson's Promenade, where long rows of trees with crew cuts languish in the riverine nebula. It flows under the bridges where homeless people deposit their human waste as grey crows caw above the murky water like false demiurges. It flows by me as I wait for the city van to the rain-eroded neighbourhood of Širokača.

Quiet and lazy flows the Miljacka through our grassy dreams.

The sky bends towards the river bottom at the concrete weirs, hydraulic jump keeps debris floating in the bubbling froth. Sitting on the stone retaining wall, dressed in camo fatigues, an amputee without a leg is fishing for scrawny barbell. He smokes soft pack Drinas with his crippled fingers, with his left hand he holds the rod and he stares at its tip. A tram roars by and he is struck by the odour of processed fuel oil and melting asphalt, the warm breath of civilisation on the march which fills white and blue shopping bags with free air, until they hover like shell-shocked souls.

Quiet and lazy flows the Miljacka, like Guadalquivir, through our grassy dreams. The impossible endures, but the peacetime Golgotha, too, is ceaseless.

Black Hen

It was during the heaviest bombing of Cazin. Aeroplanes of the former Yugoslav People's army circled above incandescent roofs, diligently dropping their payloads onto the civilian targets and the odd military one below. The town was splendidly streaked with greenery, and it may have looked like a living Persian rug with slouching human beings hastily moving through its winding streets, seldom training their gazes at the sky, for there was nothing overhead except the metal heralds of certain death.

Murderous *hogs* and cluster bombs rained down from the kingdom of heaven in unpredictable intervals. Everyone was a Nostradamus or Tiresias of Thebes, everyone divined and prophesied for others, but no one was able to help himself. The hogs weighed up to 500 kg. They would often miss their target – the iron works where ammunition and mortar shells were produced – and create regular craters in the nearby bogs. Rainwater would fill those enormous sinkholes – deep enough to swallow a decently sized two-storey house –turning them into lifeless artificial lakes, muddy eyes of the meadow. One hog fell on Villa Seth, tearing it off the adjacent house it had been glued to with surgical precision. The ground floor of that other house housed Café Alf, which persevered, steadfast and lonely, like a drunken windmill.

When it relieved itself of its payload, the plane would produce a sound similar to the groaning of an invisible Sci-Fi horror monster that some director still hasn't decided to show us. Cluster bombs emitted a different sound, a continuous melody of celestial flies unzipping, caesarean sections opening in the sky and raining thousands of bomblets. Some went off immediately, others had attractive ribbons and were booby traps for children and curious adults. Psychological warfare experts still hadn't appeared in our midst. An elderly pensioner with a socialist-era swag belly underneath a white vest was starting a fire in his summer kitchen stove one morning, and flew straight to heaven thanks to a cluster package.

Azra's next door neighbour came from the frontline, found a *toy* in his garden right next to Azra's house, and pulled the ribbon. Two metal balls went through the orange curtain on her window and landed on the soft surface of the sofa, now lit by two new beams of daylight. They looked pathetic and benign, these instruments of death: devoid of kinetic energy they could only serve as a substitute for children's marbles.

Azra's parents had a wooden chicken coop behind their house, and kept some ten chickens. Famine reduced their numbers till only two completely black silkies remained. As black as the bottom of an anthracite mine. Even their beaks and feet were black. One soon succumbed to wartime psychosis, her nerves and heart didn't weather out, and she passed on to the chicken Valhalla. The last hen, bereft of her mate, fell ill like in a *Sevdalinka* ballad with an unhappy ending. Azra's parents moved her inside, fed her the best food they had. They crushed pills and fed her the powder mixed with corn-meal. I'd always hated feathery creatures because when I was a child a rooster came at me from behind and jumped on my back.

The black hen blinked with its dark eyelids, staring in amazement at the massive china cabinet with cobalt vases and souvenir plates, and the aerial – that crown of the telly with its radial tentacles. The perfect cosmos of a nice family home. The care afforded to the bird by Azra's parents, good middle-aged people, was bizarre and alien to me, because it seemed that outside the entire universe and all the parallel worlds were on fire. I despised them a little for it, too. I was high on a childish sort of patriotism; I naively thought that my commitment in battle could have an effect on wartime reality. Their civilian reality seemed almost insane to me. To care for a sooty hen when there were thousands of dead and wounded around. To take its temperature, brew tea for it, keep it in the sitting room like a family member. Pure civilian insanity.

* * *

The black hen died so I would remember it someday
Ten years after, I know why they cared for it
I flick through my memory full of dead faces
With words I try to paint a sphere of warmth
That existed during those forty-four months of life under pressure
To wrest myself from the desire for my words to be bloody and my tongue a blade
To find a single wartime fragment
Of unbreakable human tenderness.

Underground Warriors

'Aristotle up yer arses!' a voice shouted on the western stand, as the sky sprinkled us with holy water after yet another earthly defeat.

Golden-locked angels were peeing on us, their immortal dolled-up faces in tears. A new swig of bile slid down the throat of a fictional nation. The pitch was slippery, the sky like the eye of an ox. Over 30,000 spectators on the stands. The Greeks won 1:0. I was awesomely desperate, like the rest of the rain-soaked Bosnian rubble leaving the Koševo stadium in amoeboid files, spitting and cussing, squeezing into the icy busses whose windows were fogged with condensed breath. Like ants marching into the carapace of a decayed insect. Off they went to their musty misty towns, sad toponyms on the banks of swollen rivers. To their dales overcast with tampons of black-grey clouds poked in the belly by cold chimneys of small red brick. Those rockets that would never take off towards the outer space were now deep slender wells for weary birds to find their graves in, for the chronicles of mud & rot to deposit at the bottom. Crows circled the spires, their caws fractals of a lullaby to the merciless totem of chaos and disarray.

At Piki's *Kafana Praga*, I crushed a wine glass with an elongated stem. There was no pain at all. The cross-eyed barmaid, whose face was diagonally divided by a bulging gash I envied her for, took a red first aid kid from the shelf above the sink and bandaged my hand. With a buckskin towel she wiped the crimson stains off the bar and picked up the shards. We continued drinking as if nothing had happened. Two local guys who worked in Germany were at the other end of the lacquered bar, peacefully drinking their beer from pint bottles. One of them had a massive golden star and crescent pendant on his bristly chest. First I kicked them out, then had them come back in and order a round for the house.

'You a Muslim?' I asked the one with the pendant.

'I am.'

'Why aren't you at the morning prayer then?'

I hated hypocrisy more than Radovan Karadžić himself.

'Where were you whilst I was fighting the war?'

Saccharine pseudo-oriental tones, squeezed from the instruments of the "Južni Vetar" folk ensemble, were coming from the speakers.

'Yugo-Kraut cunts!'

I wanted to punch him right in the middle of the forehead. I had three hundred dead fighters in my head. The *Gastarbeiter* were as mum as mice. I brought my hand down on the glass to draw some blood. Those two guys didn't do anything wrong, it was just a devil's dance in a twilit room, moments of sound and fury that only blood could abate for a time.

Sinan Sakić – I can see a random picture of him in my mind's eye – hairy, podgy, in a drab jacket – was screaming mawkishly from the silver plastic stereo like an out of tune nightingale. His seal ring twinkled from below the ball of the coal-coloured microphone. *Sve je postalo pepeo i dim..*, everything has turned to smoke and ash, a nuclear holocaust took place in his song, and there's nothing left to snivel for after the end of the world. Smoke and ash – like when a plank hovel is burnt to the ground.

The barmaid was squeezed into metallic black leather trousers. She had long legs and an exquisite bum. The strabismus and the crisp scar only amplified her brutal sex appeal. I got on my bike more sober than I was when I arrived at Piki's. Beating underneath my bandage was the hidden heart of my hand. Now the broad asphalt road looked like a New York avenue, partly because I was drunk, and partly because I'd spent the war in the mid-wood's twilight and the meadow's dawn. Meho Bajrić was riding his MZ motorbike behind me.

'No worries, mate, I'm lighting your way.'

A long blade of light sliced the darkness in front of me. Above Ćojluk Hill the sky was turning clear and the Lilliputian stars faded. Up there in the woods, the dugouts camouflaged with plants and rotten leaves were slowly turning into mould. Feral dogs slept; spirits of the forest howled in them. Slimy, smelly mushrooms sprouted on the breastwork logs. A green layer of moss and lichen covered the rocks in the trenches. The mouths of oxidised casings were filling with black soil. In the moonlight, the phosphorous slugs of tracer rounds glowed like lost gems. The soldiers' underworld set out to return to nature, relieved of the pressure of the iron wheel of history. Dugouts are, after all, just dank pits in the ground. Time was when we moved about in them like condensed wisps of flesh and bone.

That evening I was sitting on the terrace of Café Kavez. People were promenading along unlit pavements that were giving off the day's heat. Stormy clouds swished through the atmosphere. The air smelt of beer and cognac. I was tanking up with canned Karlovačko beer. Burst bulbs in the white orbs of the street lights, small worlds of jade blown by bullets and shrapnel, were agape in the electric air.

'I wish another war broke out, so I can get killed again,' Kiro said.

'Yes, I would do anything for war,' I sang.

A hot shower was *darning the sky to the earth*.

The dark grey mushrooms of umbrellas were passing by, grazing each other.

People looked and acted quite civil.

Clumps of dust shrank before wet salvos and smelt like a desiccated tortoise carapace.

The neon café sign flickered under low voltage.

And the night picked us up as if with the giant shovel of a hero of labour.

Tinned People

1.

Dusk drops on the neighbourhood of Podgaj like in the pulps. It trickles down the slopes of Mt Trebević carrying the embryos of the dreams people dreamt in their family homes, huddled together as if they were afraid they'd otherwise be swept up by the December northerly that strews dry crystals of snow from his wizard palms. The nearby atomic shelter grounds are fenced with wire. Inside the wire grow shady spruces, their boughs untouchable, they keep court just below the sky where woodpeckers peck at their bark looking for frozen grubs, and magpies in their Newcastle F.C. bibs chatter jocosely.

Darkness descends on Podgaj bringing prosaic dreams that ring in the hollow heads of the tinned people.

'Have you got parents?'

That was the first question my future landlord Mehmed asked. Born in 1936 in a small town in east Bosnia. Retired as a foreman in a woodworking shop. Worked all over the former country. Pension: 250 Bosnian marks. He had even worked on the awning of the Bratstvo FC stadium in my hometown. Height: 191 cm. Weight: 100 kg. Massive belly. Good teeth, no prostheses. Non-drinker due to high blood pressure caused by a fatty diet and corpulence. Afraid of dying, like every man alive. During the negotiations his wife Asija was taciturn and wise, and she served us sweets and juice made from concentrate. They are both grey, she suffers from spondylosis she developed by sleeping in the cellar during the weeks of heavy shelling. An hour and a half passed in meandering talk till Mehmed finally spat out the price and the terms of the oral tenancy agreement, which I was to abide by without exceptions. The ground floor flat was one hundred and sixty marks because I was to occupy it alone, normally it was meant for two and cost two hundred because there were two beds in the bedroom. A hundred marks per bed.

'The alley is seventy-two point five metres long.'

That was Mehmed's second sentence.

2.

In front of my double-pane windows grows a conifer tree whose name I don't know. I part the curtains emblazoned with swans, flaming flowers and intricate arabesques, and I look at its crown to see if a southerly is blowing or if wet snow has already fallen copiously. The windows are fitted with green fabric blinds and a strange latch consisting of metal hooks which end in black tokens the size of a five dinar coin. Around the tree bends a narrow strip of soil that stretches along the length of the house, that's where Asija carefully grows red and ochre marigolds. They bloom till late autumn. When they wilt, frosty weather sets in and winter begins. The flower then turns to shapeless mush, wizens and falls to the ground.

This moving description of scenery is spoilt by the heated argument coming from the adjacent house that is glued to ours like a Siamese twin. Body to body. Sometimes, as I lie in bed, a dry senile cough that tears the lungs reaches me from beyond the wall. I think about my own death then.

The boundaries of our manor are delineated by a wrought iron fence coated with silver protective paint. The landlord repeats the painting ritual every time imaginary swallows return, which is whenever he decides spring has arrived. First he thoroughly scrubs the fence with a steel brush, then he meticulously layers coats of paint, enraptured, dressed in a blue work jacket. Below our borders is a paved dead end. Across the road, from behind the neighbours' gates, juts out the roof of a house that has sunk deep below the street level. This is because houses here were built on the slope stretching down towards the city centre. Like my conifer, the roof tiles of the sunken house detect weather changes, rain or snow. Above the roofline shine the many-coloured lights of the far end of the city, dominated by the phosphorescent green logo of the company *Merkur*, stuck on the top of a high-rise. The high-rise has a mate, they are called Momo and Uzeir, the famous buildings from wartime footage, ablaze while tracers from anti-aircraft guns plunged into them.

'Beeeerrrrriiiiiiiiiiiiiinnn!!' I must have heard the voice calling from the porch of the sunken house a billion times.

This usually happened during the most pleasant moments of an afternoon kip, when a rivulet of spit ran from the corner of my mouth. The child Berin was mostly silent, only the syllables of his name stretched through the crisp air of the seventy-two-point-five-metre alley, like a droning mantra of a life of quiet desperation.

Berin is a healthy, self-effacing six-year-old boy. His older sister, a girl with the face of a likeable recalcitrant, milky complexion and a somewhat attractive body, one day emerged from a yellow VW Golf Mk2 with a belly up to her chin. She'd just finished secondary school. After a while she came again with the baby in her arms and its dad, and then disappeared. She probably moved to some neighbourhood not a smidgen more exciting than this clump of dozing houses in the prairie.

'Looks like it's about to rain, doesn't it ...' I hear Asija speaking from the window just above my ground floor.

'The wind has stopped, and the sky is black over Ilidža,' a female voice replies from Berin's house after some consideration.

'It would do us good, it's been hot these days, hasn't it?'

'You can't breathe properly.'

'Mehmed and I come out on the balcony at dusk, to catch some breeze from the mountain.'

'Oh, well, let it rain, it's time it did.'

'I've got this plum sapling, it's starting to wilt. I keep watering it, but nothing.'

'This is a Judgment Day heat wave.'

'To think, last January walnut trees blossomed in Pofalići.'

'Nothing's right and proper anymore.'

'Nothing, right you are.'

Asija shuts the window. Her grey-haired neighbour, whom she was just speaking to, is squatting below the roof of her stoop, combing the sheep wool from a pillow. This skill is passed on from generation to generation. The silence is seldom interrupted by the out-of-tune engine of a car buzzing below my open window. Yes, I wish it rained now.

3.

Here, time stopped a long time ago. *Today, the streets remember that they were fields one day*. People, motions, greetings, faces, houses, plants, cars, bicycles, clothes, everything has been salted down and slowed for decades back, and front. Children come down into the city for school, adults for work, old people when they must go to hospital. The Roma, bent double like clothes-hanger hooks, carry Big Shopper bags on their backs and hawk their wares. They stop at people's gates, and women come out and buy low quality bed-sheets and clothes from China and Turkey. The local corner shops carry bread, milk, coffee, cigarettes, fruit and veg.

'Potatoes! Peppers! Tomatoes! Cabbage!' bark the vendors from their lorries as they park them in the middle of the street.

Home delivery of foodstuffs here is impressive. From the boot of an Astra caravan a man takes out plastic basins and in them chunks of petrified cheese surrounded by a cloudy film rippling on the surface of curdled water, and offers them to a gaggle of women for degustation. Commerce continues, goods are weighed by eyeballing, or using rigged scales. Citizen Dennis Tito has been to space – who gives half a scratch on the ball-sack about measuring devices from Before Christ?

Coal is unloaded in front of gardens.

'Half a tonne,' says the coalman, rakishly leaning his elbow on the side panel.

The customer weighs with his eye, a few larger chunks of coal are chucked onto the pile, and everyone's seemingly happy, the coalmen above all.

When I head down to the city around eleven in the morning, ten houses down the alley I see a middle-aged woman in a concrete yard drinking coffee, annihilating cigarettes like a chimp wipes out his mate's lice. The bags sag under her eyes like the balls of a mangy dog. She's a castaway, and as soon as she gets up she desperately needs to grab hold of something, a coffee cup and the filter of a soft-pack Drina. That is the galactic centre around which spins her hair, her eyes, her rotting teeth, shoulders, neck, her entire blobby body. She doesn't complain about her digestive karma, she is an intestinal biped with a cigarette slit on her face.

Coffee is slurped long, meticulously. Nicotine-stained fingers clutch filters. At night, a barbecue is lit. Lard sizzles in ćevapi and sausages, hunger is a cosmic problem, food is an earthly comfort. Animal protein is burnt at an inhumane rate. People pensively sink into the piles that are their own bodies. In the morning they cough up half-digested Drina butts, hurl beef lard. People here die of heart-attacks, lung cancer, colon cancer, stomach cancer. "One dies of death," is the folk explanation. One has to *be dying* of something. The afterlife is a life of abundance, orgies, streams of alcohol, ciga-rillos. Emulsions from beyond. One goes down to the city for the birth of a child or a funeral. Time here is embalmed like the face of Ramses II. The Lord has adjourned the game and enveloped his final move. We know what it is. Good night, tinned people!

Eden Ghetto

One pleasant May morning, Đidan Šarić popped down the sports shop to pick up a nickel-plated trophy cup with a brass-coated pedestal engraved with: Bosniak Footbal Club Željezničar (Bos. Krupa), Champions of the Second Cantonal League of the Una-Sana Canton 1996/1997. He put his sporting grail under his arm and waddled off to his restaurant at the railway station to bless the loving cup with spritzer.

'Đidan, what's the score?' Bebo Točak hollers down the street.

'Three to nil for Željo.'

'The ref's been bought and sold?'

'Only fair play, no one can touch us,' replies Đidan.

'You take me for a fool,' Bebo recites his favourite saying through laughter.

'You'll be playing bush league for a while longer.'

Đidan was the owner of Šarić Company, and the director of the club. Putak was the manager and star player. Ševa was the bursar. Zilho, the youngest and strongest of the Šarić brothers, was the ultras' leader.

Željo's stadium was built on a kilometres-long eyot formed by the Una and its tributary the Krušnica. Right next to it was the stadium of the older club, Bratstvo FC, larger than Željo's by a third, with a red Tartan track. Bratstvo FC always competed a league or two above Little Željo, their pet name for the local namesake of the much more famous club from Sarajevo. When they would meet in the cup it would make for an unforgettable local derby that usually ended in a mass brawl celebrating the immortality of class struggle.

The concrete western stand at the stadium of the more affluent team, roofed with corrugated sheet metal, could take up to seven hundred well-packed spectators. Half the stand was terraces, the other half was decorated with white and blue seats, the colours of the club. During the war these two playing fields were on no man's land. There were no stands on Željo's ground, just an iron fence that fulfilled the role of seating. Out-line was only a metre and a half from the "eastern stand", so every spectator could reach out and touch the linesman. Below their tin chasses, both the home and away team benches were made out of uncomfortable wooden slats. The fourth official had a two-seat booth. Grass never grew in the goal area, the rain would turn the box into a puddle of mud where the net-keeper would wade like a flame-red flamingo.

The transfer window for the upcoming season had started in early autumn, and the former goalkeeper of Krajina FC, forty-one-year-old Omanović, arrived as a great reinforcement. His grey-streaked mullet, a fashion imported from the DDR Liga, would flutter in Željo's penalty box when he paraded and parried. When he caught the ball, his ageing yet still nimble body would slam onto the ground. He would get up quickly, dust off his jersey with his gloves and kick the ball up field. The negotiations were less than smooth, because Gomila FC from the village of Stijena had offered the veteran a wall unit to join them. When he heard that, Đidan squeezed his own offer through clenched teeth, like Marlon Brando.

'We'll give you a washing machine on top of the wall unit.'

The contract was signed there and then.

Salih, a relative of the Šarić family, a pot-bellied, bow-legged, tonsured striker proficient at village-league-style dribbling, was the team's top scorer. A few players carried shrapnel fragments in their legs as wartime mementos. Back in 1997, Coubertin's Olympic spirit still existed.

The aroma of roast lamb pushed onwards from behind the locker room, four ruminants were rotating on freshly pared spits. Cases of pint beer bottles were cooling in the nearby river Krušnica, tied to a willow tree with telephone wire. The feast was meant for the players of both teams. The match against Radnički FC from the village of Zdena, Sanski Most municipality, started at two. Three hundred and fifty of us were leaning on our elbows against the fence, watching the derby of the week, in which Željezničar needed to win by a difference of three goals in order to also win the championship.

When they saw the lamb and the beer, the away team weren't too committed and aggressive on the pitch. The referee seemed tipsy. Steward Meho Bajrić walked along the touchline leaning sideways, a pink ribbon round his left bicep and a transparent bottle of rakia in his right hand. Zilho was running along the home team's goal line like an ecstatic chicken waving a giant club flag made for the occasion. He was tailed by children bearing smaller standards.

The ultras were behind the opposition goal. They pelted the keeper with coins and beer bottles, cursing all his kith and kin, which forced him to stand at the far end of the penalty box. Every time the ball crossed the centre line into the enemy half, the goal hung in the air. Next came a deep cross towards the bouquet of players in the penalty area trying to elbow their way to a good striking position – Željezničar subscribed to a distinctly English school of football.

A minute before the end, at 2:0 for Željezničar, the pot-bellied striker was fouled and the ref awarded a penalty kick. Putak, like Ruud Gullit, brought himself on. He was wearing a dark blue shirt with the number ten, like all the brainy players, and he set the ball onto the circle of lime powder. He was the undisputed leader of the team. At over forty, he was still able to dribble his way past three opposing defenders.

The Radnički goalkeeper gestured Putak to shoot for the lower right corner. The ball smashed into the indicated spot. Three hundred and fifty people leapt upwards, gravity was momentarily vanquished. As we levitated with our arms raised in a V for victory, nothing could be heard over our roaring. We fell onto the grass, and the ref disallowed the goal for encroachment.

'Dule, fuckin' 'ell, this isn't what we agreed!' Putak yelled at the referee.

'Oi, ref, come on, it's a goal!' shouted the opposing goalkeeper.

But Dule was as unyielding as the Caesar's downward pointing thumb.

'The ref is a wanker, oh o-o-o-oh!' echoed through the stadium.

Meho Bajrić came running onto the pitch, cursing the bones of the ref's dead mother.

Dule, surrounded by players from both teams, his brain addled with alcohol, ran backwards towards the fourth official who played a UN observer zealously counting the shells fired, caring not one bit about who fired them at whom.

Đidan pacified the spectators. His face morose, he spread his arms to the sky in resignation.

The penalty was taken again.

With the studs of his boots Putak stomped down the penalty spot and placed the ball. He rakishly squirted a jet of spit through his teeth.

He took a running start, halfway to the ball he feinted, and the boy on the platform was already putting the wooden panel with the number three onto the scoreboard. The Željezničar players swan dived, the cup was gleaming on a small table draped with the flag with the shield and fleurs-de-lys. The ball was kicked up into the ozone-rich sky. A breeze was blowing, carrying the heavy breath of the floating reeds, weeds and fish from the Krušnica.

The football is a round celestial body with which godlike mortals amuse themselves on the trimmed shoots of chlorophyll clouds.

Pocket Odyssey

AROMAS

The engine of life never idles on Kaiserstraße in Frankfurt. The speed with which sequences of reality take turns before my eyes is worthy of the chaos billowing up in a droplet of pond water under the microscope slide. Perpendicular to this street runs Elbestraße, where the cheap Hotel Aba, that used to be a brothel, is situated.

The whole area is a red-light district in the city centre, a colossal retort mixing a multitude of races, nations and tongues into a single concoction. In an area of half a square metre you can hear vowels and consonants from about a dozen languages. Everything is garish and aglitter, heavy oriental scents permeate the air. Polyphemus's heart of purple neon beats on the façades of buildings, curtains of glittery thread hang above the signs of night bars, brothels, porno cinemas and sex shops. In between these houses of carnal pleasures are chains of cheap Bella Italia pizzerias, Turkish kebab spits spinning next to incandescent coils like those in an electric heater. You can even order *cevapcici*.

Then there are the rows of African, Iranian and Pakistani shops from which emanate the aromas of non-European spices. There I can feel the breath of the faraway cities I've visited thanks to the cathode tube or the atlas.

I can see the kitchens where unimaginable dishes, wholly alien to the taste buds of a regular Balkan carnivore, simmer, steam and burn. Battered crickets in cuttle oil, armadillo chops, braised opossum with desert spinach and cactus stuffed with flambéd bananas are some of the dishes I imagine as I breathe the bombastic molecules of spice from the lands found in the atlas.

The spicy spectre haunts Frankfurt like flocks of aeroplanes circling above the local airport that looks like the Starship Enterprise, steered by the steady hand of Captain Picard. I half expect to see him just as he utters the mythical sentence: "Space, the final frontier". The airport would take off from the ashen concrete and become a WARP-driven spaceship. Walking through the red-light quarter I realise that Star Trek exists in this very district and one should look no further for an arabesque of cultures and civilisations, because Borges's metaphoric tiger, the reflection of the Other, wanders through this perfectly orderly immigrant ghetto.

CASTLE OF NOTHINGNESS

What my eye sees as El Dorado in a split second turns into a dystopian image of human life. Opposite the hotel Aba in which we're staying, drug addicts hang about 0–24 in front of the drug treatment service. In the morning they are given clean syringes, bandages and vitamin drinks. A visit to the Garden of Eden is ten or twenty euros, depending on the price of the hit.

A hologram in a moto jacket frantically plays ska on a two-string guitar, others smoke weed, swallow pills and beer, languish on the asphalt like viruses in bloody spittle.

From the frail syringes heroin immigrates into their bloodstream. They sleep sheathed in their jackets like mayfly larvae in their husks of grit. Every hour or two, a green and white police car patrols the streets like a detail of guards in a concentration camp. In the morning a game is played: search for lost bits of skunk. Players are those who can still stand on their feet. Fights among the addicts are a common occurrence. I watched when a tiny moustachioed fellow attacked a swarthy long-haired Ausländer. He put up a kickboxing guard, flailed his legs wildly in front of the face of his adversary who calmly ignored him. A group of aimless walkers gathered around them trying to pacify them. Mr Tash was exceedingly worked up and aggressive, whereas the foreigner, in a submissive pose, did not exactly radiate strength and power. The whole thing finished when the frail German fell onto the pavement and chucked his liver out, then cried a torrent whilst conferring with creatures hovering in thin air, visible to him only. They soon made peace with one another. They were so effete their fight looked like ballet of drunken cockerels. The addicts' solidarity was strong, even in conflict; nothing could come between them and their common pursuit of slow death.

These scuffles never varied in frequency, nor did the script ever change, only the protagonists did. Sadness and disgust blended inside me, and after two days I was no longer sure how I felt about these people stuck halfway between zombies and manic street preachers.

Dragan and I spotted all the peculiar characters, gave them nick-names. Every night we would buy a few beers at the nearby Turkish shop and chug leaning our elbows against a metal distribution cabinet in front of the entrance to the hotel. From the other side of the cabinet miniature people in tattered clothes approached us and slumped to the foot of the metal box. I leaned over and saw the husk of a woman trying, and failing, to find a vein on her arm. A car drove past and she guided her hand by the light of the headlamps. When she found the blue path to heaven and took care of business, she fell into a coma. A tall girl in a raincoat walked up to her. Her features retained traces of beauty. She shouted something in German, but I only remembered the name of her wasted friend. It was Eli. I was overcome by a sorrow not of this world. On the face of the girl in the raincoat only the nose remained life-sized, and looked more than grotesque. Her cheek bones deformed, her chin assumed the shape of an office drawer. Her clasped jaws were pulled apart by gravity. On each side of her nose her eyes reflected the sceneries of infernal worlds in which a measureless NOTHING reigned supreme.

WHORES

Prostitutes constituted a special caste in the red district. One bow-legged whore in long leather boots paraded by every night. Every time she walked past I was struck by a saturated odour of something unknown and terrible, something I can compare only to the smell of a house long abandoned by human beings during wartime. Dragan said it was the smell of her body. We scanned two more with gelatinous globs of silicone between which their sternums could be made out, signalling that they were after all living beings. Their powdered faces inevitably looked like casts of their former faces. The bionic masks paced, smoked cigarettes and offered their services. It was hard to gauge the age of the two walking, swollen, shrivelled crinolines, routinely and mercilessly worn down by life, like it's hard to tell the age of a stuffed pet. Those humanoid faces were sensors of the millennial animaline struggle for existence. Tissue annealed in lust for life was stretched over her jutting cheekbones. Prostitutes are not any kind of fallen muses, or cherubs shot down onto the piss-stained pavement, they are three-dimensional creatures into whose souls I dare not take a peek, for pure fear.

If I eschew the romanticist vantage point, I can imagine a picture in which prostitutes take off their leather gowns and clad themselves in the prepartum placenta of the night. If the Communist Manifesto should gain the upper hand over the Book of Revelations, the day after the Day of Judgment prostitutes will be raping Johns, celebrating the beginning of the anal revolution, when the prisoners of want arise.

SURROGATES

Laid out on pink silk in the windows of sex shops were the battle ranks of sex utensils: rubber dildos, metal and plastic vibrators, normal to king size. In addition to standard shapes, also on display were models like the one resembling an enormous playing card spade, or the one that was over a metre long and looked like a spear with spiked balls and a tapering tip. A monstrous harpoon for impaling vaginas of cosmic proportions. There were also the Japanese anal beads, leather whips with lead balls at the end of the thongs, narrow-gauge fannies, cock rings, chrome-plated handcuffs, SM uniforms, Japanese inflatable dolls and porno VHS tapes.

The prices of gas guns in army and firearms shops ranged from 77 to 250 euros. From behind the curtains of the shop windows jutted out the barrels of carbines, shotguns, hunting and trophy pieces, a metaphor of Thanatos in the fusty erotic setting. Some hundred paces away sprouted up a troop of sparkling skyscrapers in the banking district. We wandered through the financial scenery and came upon a giant construction site, where a massive drill was rhythmically rising up into the sky and sticking into the ground. The iron finger of a demiurge bored deep into the soil, making pits for the steel anchor cages of the solitaire, an un-fuck-with-able peg-leg striding down the boulevard of broken dreams.

faruk sehic and the blackhearts

"Life is a popular phenomenon"
Stevan Tontić

VOL. 1

Yesterday morning Roša shot a young rabbit. Its coat was wet, combed by dew. Its nose warm and bloody. A purple tongue was hanging from under it, slowly assuming the colour of the sky. We roasted the kill before the flayed carcase could even drain out. The meat was as sweet as an Una grayling. After the meal we lapped up rainwater that had accumulated in a lorry tyre from our palms. We smoked a cigarette for desert. Flies were laying white eggs on the rabbit's skin mucous with curdled blood that had been tossed by the extinguished fire. I looked at the glaring sphere at its zenith. Dazed by the sun, I lowered my gaze to the green hillocks overgrown with grass that reached a man's chest. A raven's wing flapped through the air as clear as the mountain crystal. A feather, black with a greasy sheen in all the colours of the rainbow, spiralled to the ground wet from last night's rain. A bad omen in a horror film. Žile spat three times towards the bird, to ward off the devil's messenger.

''Ere comes Three Fingers!'

'Food's comin'!'

'What did you bring us? Is it beans?'

'Macaroni,' replies Three Fingers.

'With what?' Ćerim looks at Roša.

'Chef's droppings!' Roša replies off the cuff.

Three Fingers is a forty-year-old of medium height, with a brown moustache and wild, dishevelled hair. On his right hand, with which he holds the reins, he's missing two fingers.

'Hey, Three Fingers, you old rake, kiss a cock the size of a snake,' shouts Zgemba.

'Go on, take the piss. But remember, if not for me you'd be eating barren ewe cock stew. Woah, lad, eeeasy now, there…' Three Fingers steers his black steed, whose ribs look like the futtocks of a rotten lifeboat.

The cart passes along the boundary of a plot of land and the bramble bushes and nettle below.

'What's up at the HQ?' Žile asks.

''Ow's the commander? 'As 'e plumped up? 'As 'e been shaggin' regularly?'

'Is there any meat in the mac?'

'Steady on, lads, it's not our last day on earth,' Three Fingers puts up resistance.

He gets off his throne, a car seat mounted at the front of the cart, to which he ties the reins. He looks at the collapsible table with some plastic yoghurt cups, now empty of coffee. We are standing round the table, Zgemba, Žile, Ćerim, Roša and me.

'Go on, 'ave a fag,' Ćerim offers Three Fingers a cigarette.

Three Fingers licks the fragrant cigarette paper, Ćerim flicks the lighter.

I light up a Drina light, hunch down and stand in front of the shop window in which swim carp, Californian trout and eel. I stare at the fish eyes. The bottom of the aquarium is strewn with road gravel. Two lobsters are resting on the gravel, their pincers tied with heavy fishing line. Enter Smajo, street piss artist extraordinaire, his face plum-coloured from drink. He hands the fishmonger some copper pieces. The fishmonger fills him a half-litre bottle with synthetic loza. Seen through the aquarium, Smajo's head becomes a black stain. His body shrinks and rocks like on the gibbet. The trout swiftly slice the water like silver spindles, whirling up the filthy froth that cleaves to the glass walls of the piscine gulag.

Smajo winks and the gear stick knob in his throat slides up and down, lubricated with the fiery liquid. He puts the bottle into the pocket of his windcheater. He crosses Ferhadija street and sits on a green bench. The wind from Marshall Tito street is the whistles of the singed Partisan souls being recycled inside the metal burner wheel of the Eternal Flame monument ardent in their honour in the centre of Sarajevo. He hawks and spits onto the granite cobbles. The spittle stretches like a yo-yo and bounces back to his bristly beard which starts just below his eye-bags, like the youngest and meanest of the Dalton brothers.

Željko is slobbering down the neck of a pint bottle. Papa is puffing on a soft-pack Drina. The sun pops into the treetop, the interplay of light and leaf acts as a laterna magica projecting onto their wrinkled clothes. After a few draughts Smajo's head dives between his knees and he falls asleep. The other two take his rakia, push him onto the grass behind their backs. Smajo mumbles in a trans-tongue, hisses cracking curses. His skull lies on the sods of turf like a football made out of holey socks. Beads of sweat billow on his brow, burst, and the trickles of the salty excretion run towards his unibrow, reminiscent of Frida Kahlo's. Ants climb up his ear lobe. With their antennae they gauge the hairs and the petrified sebum on his greasy skin.

Željko throws up, wipes yellow slime off his lips. Trouser legs hurtle by his face. Papa takes a good swig from the bottle and the webs of capillaries on his nose flare up vermillion. A pair of filthy jeans approaches, atop the trunk an angry head, greasy sticky hair, mouth agape.

'Željko, fuck you and all of yours, except Fabijan! Your pension arrived, you stood everyone a drink but me,' hisses the drunken, sticky-maned woman.

'Piss off… wazzock!'

She pushes her way through the throngs of people and parks next to a textile shop window. When somebody passes by her she puts on the grimace of a Biblical martyr from religious brochures, stretches out a hand and begs for a mark. At times her words resurrect in the mind of a random philanthropist or a Tartuffe, and he turns them into small change. If she fails to ponce some off, her face crumples up and she waves her piss-stained palm.

'Cuntin' 'ell! Fuck me life!'

Solemnly flourishing his tail, the alpha carp hovers in the middle of the shop window. Scales the size of a human nail gleam in the light of the quartz lamp. In his belly daydreams a miniature Jonah. Rejected by mortal men and the All-Wise alike, he believes in the frail power of the forces of good. This thought of mine, which has taken on prophetic overtones, drips from the fish's anus.

VOL. 3

'Can you 'magine, that idiot of a commander 'ad a plaster boot cast for 'im. 'E can't walk in bandages. 'E puts on 'is proper boot, then the pot over it. 'Is foot is massive, like Big Foot's,' Žile is telling Three Fingers.

'Big who?' enquires Three Fingers.

'Cast boot up 'is mum's fanny!' adds Roša 'we've been 'ere for three days without any water, and 'e's collectin' fashion accessories.'

'Come on, lads, don't be so harsh on the commander. He's all right when he sleeps, causes no trouble,' says Three Digits.

The crippled driver unloads the tin food container from the back of his cart.

'Cooks ought to be court-martialled and shot, they steal and squirrel stuff away,' says Zgemba.

'Logisticians are apt to get KIA by heart attack from all the drink and meze,' concludes Roša.

'The commander's adjutant ate three packets of Danish Feta, his kidneys collapsed, the man's in intensive in Bihać now!' says Ćerim.

'Three Fingers, you're one of their narks, you're going to grass on us,' says Zgemba.

'May I go blind if I do!'

'Yeah, right. All you logisticians are the same,' Ćerim supports Zgemba.

'I swear by me children, I'm as right as a pie!'

Zgemba produces an M-75 hand grenade, rips out the safety pin and tosses it onto the table. Three Fingers zooms down the berm into the brambles. Everyone has hit the deck, but Zgemba is still standing. The grenade is spinning among the upturned yoghurt cups bleeding dregs of roasted rye coffee. He picks up

164

the Kinder egg, as we used to call this type of grenade, unscrews it open and shows us the inside with the firing pin removed. The fright almost killed us during those five or six seconds. We laugh. A soiled Three Fingers, covered in scuffs and scratches, curses mothers, curses stars and galaxies. He hops into the seat of his cart.

'I will file a complaint at the HQ!'

'Take yer three fingers and stick 'em up yer arse!' shouts Zgemba.

He screws the lid shorn of the firing pin back into the body of the grenade. He pushes the safety pin through the hole, bends it on the other side.

'Shall we go hunt raven?' says Zgemba.

VOL. 4

Smajo stuttered away to have a piss in an exotic bush. Željko and Papa, two dead-weights, scarecrows in the corn, languish on the bench, sunken into their clothes. An alkie walking past in a wool coat stops in the middle of the pavement, jerks the coat off his shoulders, spreads it before his feet, takes a step, suddenly bends his knees and sits a-la-turca, like an Indian chieftain. With his watery Adriatic-blue eyes he stares at the passers-by. His hand transforms into an alms box, into a gaff of despair with which he tenaciously hooks pecuniary plankton in the air.

A street harlequin is rapping a refrain to a regiment of strollers:

"Verily our hearts are sooty from wanking whilst on tour of duty."

I get up from the neighbouring bench, bent like a sickle. I dream up an outline for a perfect book of prose about cigarettes and tobacco smoke.

Postcards from Mars

We came back from the sector facing the Autonomists, having captured Murat Hill, the first obstacle on the road to the town of Velika Kladuša. Down in the dell, among the houses, at the foot of the devil's own bump, Vejsil "Deba" Šarić was killed. Executed, with his hands tied behind his back with steel wire. Former Yugoslav Navy officer Šefko Begić, and Huse Velagić, stayed behind lying on the greasy plough-field on the plateau atop the hill, shrouded in heavy October fog.

On Murat Hill, the Autonomists' slit trenches were densely packed, barely two metres apart. They looked like children's graves. The line was virtually impenetrable. Storming over the sodden field was the only solution. My platoon was deployed at the summit Groblje, three kilometres from that part of the sector as the crow flies. The twenty-eight of us held picket setting up all-round defence in the gentle copse along which meandered a gravel road.

We listened to the entire Murat Hill operation on the radio, as if it had been a football match. Ours was a lonely position, we had no contact with other units. Nine kilometres inside enemy territory. In the event of a substantial attack, we were designated scapegoats.

After the third platoon of the first company relieved us, Mirsad Šoma was killed from behind with a hunting carbine, from a Yugoslav-made Fiat 600 that descended down the macadam road into the nearby village of Lidane. We were a well-hated occupying force.

We agreed to meet opposite Café M, by the fence behind the Cazinka department store, in the town in which we were refugees.

A green glass bottle of home-distilled rakia went from lips to lips.

We smoked Gales and Macedonian Partners.

Arif Motor, Nino, Juicy and I, warmed up by rot-gut, sang patriotic songs.

Nirvana's unplugged version of *The Man Who Sold the World* was coming from the café.

We said we'd refrain from public acts of cuntery, so we guzzled away from the boozers.

The loss of Deba was hard to get over. He was a fighter with a solid pair of bollocks on him, always had a cynical comment about the radio singing our invincible army's praises. He left behind two underage children, who he used to call his turtles.

A civpol van stopped in the street in front of the café.

The door opened, ten civ coppers in blue camo uniforms emerged.

They took their batons and started beating us for no reason at all.

I pulled my usual number, I stripped to the waist.

Tossed my jumper and jacket onto the concrete.

Dim ocean-coloured neon pulsated above the café entrance.

The tin dog-tag engraved with a fleur-de-lys and the number 03 1043 was swinging on the shoe-lace tied round my neck.

'Is that your best, cunts?'

When I fell, I felt the firmness of the asphalt on my cheek.

'God was a mushroom,' mumbled street prophet Zlaja Cile as he hurried past staring at the cardboard-coloured sky.

We were unarmed and they quickly dragged us into the car.

We drove down to the station, not fifty metres from the place where we'd been drinking.

They led us into an icy corridor, lined us up with our hands raised against the wall.

Every time I turned around to swear at them, the policeman behind me socked me in the nape.

I'd seen him around, his name was Himzo Osmanagić.

Jug-eared, with button-sized eyes beaming endemic stupidity, he had a waddling gait on account of his x-legs and excessive weight. His temples were sunken in, so his head tapered like a reamer or the helmet of the Spanish conquistadors.

I was numb with drink and I couldn't feel a thing.

They cited "singing of Autonomist songs" as grounds for arrest.

Motor wanted to speak to their commander, Asim "Hamza" Bajraktarević.

We knew Hamza would help us, he was from the town of Bužim, their brigade and ours bore the brunt of the fighting against the Autonomists.

He turned up after half an hour.

'Who told you to do over the fighters of the five 'leven brigade?'

He drew up the entire police force.

We waited for the moment to go berserk.

He ordered them to leave their weapons and Motorolas at the desk on their way out.

'Now piss off home, the lot of ya!'

The degenerates cleared the building in a file.

I wish I'd met that mutant Himzo on the frontline after the incident, I would've shot him like a cur, for the sheer pleasure of it.

A group of detained civilians were standing about at the far end of the corridor.

We started tossing empty ammunition boxes stacked up along the pale turquoise wall.

A civilian, as hirsute as Tom Selleck, tried to tidy up the scattered boxes.

Hamza kicked him in the neck.

The hairy primate returned to the pack.

The commander let us take it all out on the inventory of the police station.

We didn't want to go home. We phoned our brigade HQ and asked to speak to the brigade commander.

The van of an MP unit attached to our brigade drove past with some arrested Autonomists.

Just what the doctor ordered.

The Autonomists were in civvies.

We swore at them.

We sat on the wooden benches running along the sides of the van.

Between us and the arrestees sat the MPs.

They were neutral.

Motor put his arm round an Autonomist, head-butted him.

Blood gushed forth from the Autonomist's nose.

Facing me sat a strapping fellow of forty, the hair on his bovine head grey, his face furrowed with wrinkles and deep acne scars.

I socked him straight in the face.

He took the jabs quietly, like a fervid enemy.

Juicy and Nuno had patients of their own.

The ring on Motor's finger broke from all the chiselling.

My knuckles were bleeding.

I leaned my back against the metal side of the van and hit the prisoner in the forehead with my foot.

The policemen didn't react.

The van stopped suddenly.

The driver, Šehad, opened the door of the back compartment and asked us to stop lest the van tip over.

We were in the middle of nowhere. Murk and ashen haze lorded it over the outside world.

Exhausted by our labours we slumped onto the benches.

The prisoners were quiet, their heads cracked.

The right leg of my faux washed-out Levi's jeans I bought at the market for fifteen marks was blood-splattered up to the knee.

The thin sole of my faux Chucks fell off.

Commander Mirsad Crnkić ordered us to his office.

The prisoners were urgently transported to the brigade aid post.

We had a few shots of whisky.

The hour hand of the round clock on the wall was stuck on 1.

He gave us a packet of Marlboros each.

We explained the situation.

He excused everything except the thing with the Autonomists.

He asked if we'd taken rings off their fingers, as that was their complaint.

We hadn't, of course.

We respected him because he hadn't merged with his role in the army.

He was still a human being.

Motor asked for permission to muster up the recce company, "The Pharaohs", and torch down the police station in Cazin.

The commander calmed us down, promising he would demand an apology from the police, who we all knew tacitly supported Fikret Abdić.

He arranged for a vehicle to take us to our refugee homes…

I told all this to a stranger, who'd never been to war, as we stood at the bar in a restaurant car.

I watched as the crimson withdrew from his cheeks and his face turned pale.

'Sorry, I got carried away there for a bit,' I said.

'No bother, interesting story,' said the stranger, paid for the round of miniatures and went to his compartment, sallow-faced.

And I never even mentioned Bešić's steaming intestines, which he pushed back into his stomach ripped up by hollow-point bullets with his woollen mittens, grey-green lint sticking to the hot mucous membrane. Or the undigested bean seed coats he'd had for lunch, and now the stew was blending with blood. There was just no point in bringing that up. Bešić was subsequently nicknamed Tinman, because tiny bits of bullet jackets were coming out through the skin around his navel for months after he was wounded. *Glory, as anyone knows, is bitter stuff*, says Mishima in *The Sailor Who Fell from Grace with the Sea*.

I was afraid of sleeping, for there was no stopping the tide of wartime scenes, and nothing could stop my heart from skipping like a series of short bursts of machinegun fire.

I would often leap out of bed with my strawberry beating in my throat, turn on every light in the flat and open all the windows. My heart pulsated like a smallish supernova, and I listened to it, trying to slow down the insane tick-tockery with the sheer power of thought.

Blackbirds, oblivious to the October melancholy, languished perching on the electrical wires.

To be a yellow-beaked blackbird in a lilac bush!

The train was dancing on the tracks, massive, faster than Muhammad Ali.

Champions' League was on the following night.

There was nothing better in the whole wide world. I was sure they would play attractive, world-class football.

With the help of Xanax and lager I was going to have a vision of the razed ivory towers of the ruling elites.

The Apocalypse was going to come in the form of a photon torpedo. Without warning, without scenes of mass suffering, the Second Coming, the Beast, the screams, the ceremonies. It was going to come from all directions at once and stick into one tiny dot. My heart.

Like a Rolling Stone (the final flashback)

1.

Around half eight in the morning, on my way to the frontline, I popped down to Kafana Rogovi to see Dina. In my pocket I had three postal coupons worth a mark each, plenty to set out on a threepenny odyssey. (*I was indifferent to all crews/The bearer of Flemish wheat or English cottons/When with my haulers this uproar stopped/The rivers let me go where I wanted*). I had two hand grenades in my tactical rucksack. A 9 mm short-cartridge pistol in a holster on my belt. Is there a single boozer in the world where that ox-eyed Romani boy isn't looking at you from a cheap reproduction painting? He was sad, just like that, just like the Una was frothy and blue-green. If the eyes are the window to the soul, the lad suffered from *Weltschmerz*. I was having a cup of Turkish coffee, looking at the post office building on which fluttered the flags of the Army of Bosnia and Herzegovina, and, of course, SDA, the Bosniak nationalist party.

The boozer was slapped together with planks and roofed with tiles. A pair of bullock's horns jutted out cockily above the entrance, hence the name *Rogovi*. The interior looked decent, a framed coat of arms was hanging on the wall above the miniature bar. I had a coffee and Dina stood me a high-ball of home distilled rakia, a libation worthy of a hero.

Dina had short bleached hair, and was quite tall, sturdily built. She lived with her mother and son on the mouldy ground floor of a one-storey house. The kind of Zen and heartiness she possessed had healing properties in this hallucinogenic world. I didn't bother counting the glasses, so I didn't know how many I'd had. I produced my crumpled-up postal coupons, but Dina wouldn't let me pay. At nine o'clock, my eyes were full of haze, flickering like air off the hot asphalt. Happens when one chugs on an empty stomach. Food was always a secondary concern. I didn't want to eat, as rakia doesn't hit you quite as forcefully on a full stomach. *Better drunk than old,* or so the song would have it. Better drunk than dead. Or, better yet, better dead drunk now, than whatever happens later. I said good-bye to Dina and set out for the village of Gnjilavac, the rendezvous point for all the hitchhikers, civilian and military. There you could hitch a ride on a tractor taking dung straight into the cosmos. The potential corpse is off to the frontline.

2.

In the desert-style kafana called "The Sultan's" I quaff down a few large glasses of rot-gut. The landlord is a sluggish moustachioed fellow, his son is juggling a rubber football in front of the establishment. For a while now, there has been no vehicular traffic down the road to the village of Pištaline. I piss into a squat toilet invaded by mysterious alcohol algae. A copious stream of urine drums on the floating turds. *Piss moves in mysterious ways.* There's a war on, all that fear makes people shit a lot and forget to flush. Haply the water tank has been swept up by the wild winds of war. It's a melancholy water tank, with no water gurgling through, here in this fusty kafana on Gnjilavac Hill, hard by the brim of the world. This is the seat of the God of Ammonia. I wash my hands in the basin. I return to my table.

I light up a fag. No tractor in sight. The sun is beating straight down on the bleached asphalt. I forgot to describe my feelings. I have none, as I am pissed and I give half a horse cock about emotions. No rage, no sorrow, no despair, no numbness, no melancholia, no love, no fear, no optimism, no heroism, no patriotism, no homesickness, no fucksickness, no boredom, no resignation, no weariness, nothing. Such is my state of mind, and there is some turbulence in my head. My face is flushed with drink. I breathe hot alcohol fumes. They smell of acetone. Fat flies are trying to fly through the greasy glass. (*A black velvety jacket of brilliant flies/ Which buzz around cruel smells.*) I put out the fag in a tin ashtray. A moustachioed fellow emerges from the back room, spreading the curtain open. The worn soles of his slippers shuffle along the greasy floor.

'Lad, git inside, they're gonna start shellin'!' the Sultan nonchalantly tells the boy who then darts into the blacked-out house.

And claps his hands two or three times loudly.

I move towards the bar decorated with a wooden bowl of artificial flowers spotted with fly droppings. O, fluid essence of war, dwellest thou in the faeces of a solitary housefly?

'On tab, ok?'

'Nah. 'Ow much 'ave you got?'

'Three coupons.'

'Gimme that. You owe me four marks on top of this. I know yer mug, don't fuck me over. I've got to make a livin',' the Sultan makes sure I don't forget the debt.

I squint outside trying to get used to the light. I spit in front of my feet, spread the spittle around with my boot. Framed by her window, an elderly lady from a house opposite blows thick puffs of smoke. Her eye-bags are filled with nicotine & coffee dregs. Chance took pity on me: a horse cart slows down to a halt. The harnessed horses neigh, their muscles twitch with fatigue. A quartz-green horsefly set up shop on the croup of the leading horse. The insect looks like the Order of Merit First Class of the former SFRY.

'Where ya headed?'

'Stijena.'

I hop on and sit in the back.

'What brigade?' the driver asks me. 'Giddy up, lad!'

'511 Infantry Bosanska Krupa.'

'How's things on Ćojluk? They attackin'?'

'It's not bad.'

'This'll pass eventually, must endure.'

A fusillade of sunrays hits my nape. We are descending into a dale covered in yellow asters. The driver, a gramps with a skull-cap and a Hitler moustache, rides the brake lever. Axle squeaks. The horses, suddenly disburdened, assume a dignified gait. We ride past the mosque in Gnjilavac. Deba is buried there. Every time I pass I look at his grave that seems older as the mound settles and sinks.

'Giddy up! Lift the left, ye'r pissin' on the shaft! Giddy up, mad cunt!' the gramps lords it over the horse.

3.

We passed the villages of Polje and Čatakovići, where mighty plums grow and the rakia is godly. Then we passed Prhline and arrived in Stijena.

'Ta for the ride.'

'Good luck, lad!' says the gramps.

Now I feel thirsty. At the junction I see Hari Žutić and Ćelo Desankin. There's a butcher's shop converted to a kafana by the bus stop. I invite them for drinks. We drink pints of Bihaćko beer and chase them with counterfeit bourbon from 2 dl glasses. They're going on leave, I'm going on duty. Alcohol has brought us together; we've finally attained ethnic homogeneity! We walk out of the boozer without paying. The waiter doesn't so much as look at us, probably thanks to the barrel of my nine. Such cheekiness is in vogue. Born to be wild, and all.

I leave them in front of the Motel Horljava and press on by foot towards Pištaline. Crickets play the summer fugue in the hot grass. Blood swooshes in my temples in time with them. What an arcane union of matter and energy in nature! I've become immune to alcohol. I must've measured this road with my steps a hundred times. After some three hundred metres I stop a tractor, an IMT–539, the uncrowned king of plough fields, smallish and stocky, like the Bosnian mountain horse. As we fly downhill, the driver switches off the engine to save fuel. I hear the air swoosh as we roll on driven by inertia like Jens Weißflog, the legendary ski jumper.

In twenty minutes' time I was in Pištaline. As always, I didn't feel like going on duty. As I passed by Šoferska noć I was hoping someone would invite me in for a drink. No one did.

I lift my gaze towards the sky. It's not its fault. I put my hands in the pockets of my camo trousers. I whistle some idiotic patriotic ditty. I play pocket pool. I get off the asphalt onto a gravel road. Hand grenades are clanking in my assault rucksack. The potential corpse is off to the frontline. 'Giddy up, giddy up, mad cunt!' I drive an imaginary horse out loud. The pressure in my veins and arteries stretches my skin taut. Unrestrained shouting, however, soon becomes boring. The feeling dwindles and deflates like a bubble in white dough. I take three steps to the side. I sit on the fragrant green meadow. Up in the air, the wind blows dandelion fuzz every which way. I put my head on my rucksack. A bumblebee buzzes in the crown of a black locust tree. I close my eyes and listen to the breath of the earth in the pulsating chlorophyll of the plants. A goldfinch sings me a lullaby.

The Author

FARUK ŠEHIĆ was born in Bihać, in the Socialist Federal Republic of Yugoslavia. Until the outbreak of war in 1992, he studied veterinary medicine in Zagreb. At that point, the then 22-year-old voluntarily joined the army of Bosnia and Herzegovina, in which he led a unit of 130 men. After the war he studied literature and has gone on to create his own literary works. Critics have hailed Šehić as the leader of the 'mangled generation' of writers born in 1970s Yugoslavia, and his books have achieved cult status with readers across the whole region. His third book *Under Pressure* (*Pod pritiskom*, 2004) was awarded the Zoro Verlag Prize. His debut novel *Quiet Flows the Una* (*Knjiga o Uni*, 2011) received the Meša Selimović Prize for the best novel published in Serbia, Bosnia and Herzegovina, Montenegro and Croatia in 2011 and the EU Prize for Literature in 2013. His most recent books are the collection of poetry entitled *My Rivers* (*Moje rijeke*, Buybook, 2014) and *Clockwork Stories* (*Priče sa satnim mehanizmom*, Buybook 2018). His books are translated into many languages. Šehić lives in Sarajevo and works as a columnist and journalist.

The Translator

MIRZA PURIĆ is a literary translator working from German and BCMS. He is a contributing editor of *EuropeNow* and in-house translator for the Sarajevo Writers' Workshop. From 2014 to 2017 he was an editor-at-large for *Asymptote*. He has published several book-length translations into BCMS, including Nathan Englander's *The Ministry of Special Cases*, Michael Köhlmeier's *Idylle mit ertrinkendem Hund* and Rabih Alameddine's *The Hakawati*. His translations into English have appeared in *Asymptote, H.O.W., EuropeNow, AGNI, PEN America, Versopolis, The Well Review* and elsewhere. His co-translation, with Ellen Elias-Bursać, of Miljenko Jergović's story collection *Inshallah, Madonna, Inshallah*, will be released in 2020 by Archipelago Books.

Many thanks to all our supporters on Kickstarter
who made the translation and publication of this book possible,
especially:

MATTHEW BATES

THE MAYOR OF BOSANSKA KRUPA

WAYLES BROWNE

NATASHA CHISDES

ADNAN ČIŠIJA

ZLATKO ĆORALIĆ

KATHRIN EHRKE

AMER HADŽIHASANOVIĆ

COLIN HARRIS

SAQIB HASAN

ALEKSANDAR HEMON

ALMA KARUV

KAPKA KASSABOVA

NICK KENT

IVICA LEKIĆ

EVE LEIGH

ROMA GONZÁLEZ MARTÍNEZ

BERTRAND MONTEL

KEMAL NIKŠIĆ

MARTA NOVOVIĆ

DAVID PIGOTT

INGRID SAGER

NAĐA ŠEHIĆ

MICHAEL TATE

CLIFF WU

CHRISTINA P. ZORIĆ